Love many things,
for therein lies the true strength,
and whosoever loves much performs much,
and can accomplish much, and what is done in love is done well.

—VINCENT VAN GOGH

No love allowed

KATE EVANGELISTA

SWOON READS | NEW YORK

For the future . . .
Because everybody who wants one has one.

A SWOON READS BOOK
An Imprint of Feiwel and Friends

NO LOVE ALLOWED. Copyright © 2016 by Kate Evangelista.
Excerpt from *The Way to Game the Walk of Shame* © 2016 by Jenn P. Nguyen.
All rights reserved. Printed in the United States of America by
R. R. Donnelley & Sons Company, Harrisonburg, Virginia.
For information, address Feiwel and Friends/Swoon Reads,
175 Fifth Avenue, New York, N.Y. 10010.

Our books may be purchased in bulk for promotional, educational, or
business use. Please contact your local bookseller or the Macmillan Corporate
and Premium Sales Department at (800) 221-7945, ext. 5442, or by
e-mail at MacmillanSpecialMarkets@macmillan.com.

Library of Congress Cataloging-in-Publication Data
Evangelista, Kate.
    No love allowed / Kate Evangelista.—First edition.
        pages   cm
    Summary: A wealthy boy's plan to survive the summer social season by
hiring a fake girlfriend goes in an unexpected direction when he falls in love
with bi-polar artist Didi.
    ISBN 978-1-250-07390-7 (paperback)—ISBN 978-1-250-07803-2 (e-book)
[1. Love—Fiction.   2. Manic-depressive illness—Fiction.   3. Mental
illness—Fiction.   4. Wealth—Fiction.]   I. Title.
    PZ7.E87365No 2012   [Fic]—dc23   2015013397

Book design by Liz Dresner

First Edition—2016

10   9   8   7   6   5   4   3   2

swoonreads.com

One

CALEB BARELY STIFLED a grimace.

Across the table from him, Amber burst into tears. He hated how good he had gotten at predicting when the emotional shit would hit the fan. The chin quiver, the reddening of the nose, the welling of the eyes—he had memorized all the signs. What grated most was that the skill came from years of experience. He could teach a Master's class in Jerkology. In his defense, he thought he had made things clear at the start of senior year. Amber had readily agreed to no-strings-attached fun.

The original plan was to break up with her a week before he left for Europe with his cousin Nathan. Unfortunately for him and his carefully crafted post-summer breakup speech, she had other plans. Yesterday, at her graduation after-party, she invited him out on the dock behind her house and broke his number one rule under the moonlight. If he were less messed up, he would have been happy to have someone like Amber in his life. Beautiful. Well-bred. A girl his father would approve of. Instead he kissed her on the cheek, made some excuse about running an errand, left the party, and then sent her a text asking to meet him at the country club for lunch.

He pushed the starched white napkin on his side toward her. Ignoring it, she opened the small purse she had with her and pulled out a neatly folded square of tissue. She dabbed at the corners of her eyes and sniffed. He suspected crocodile tears from the way her actions seemed so rehearsed. Each sniff and silent sob orchestrated to tug at his heart, or whatever was left inside his chest. As far as he was concerned, the muscle had been buried along with his mother all those years ago.

Tapping the table with his index finger, he admitted to himself that asking her out to lunch to break up with her might not have been the best idea. He definitely shouldn't have started the speech right after ordering a blue cheese burger and truffle fries for himself and a Caesar salad with croutons, anchovies, and dressing on the side for her. But he'd had to stop this before Amber's *feelings* dug in deeper. In his mind, he was doing her a favor.

Heads swiveled their way from curious onlookers. Since it was the weekend, the dining room was packed. Another strike against him. Caleb shut his eyes to keep from rolling them when the women began whispering. Before sundown, news would reach the farthest corners of Dodge Cove. He could see the headline in big, bold letters: FAMOUS LAWYER'S SON BREAKS UP WITH IMPORTANT CLIENT'S DAUGHTER.

"Amber," he said, his eyebrows coming together. She gasped

as if he had lobbed a grenade at her. He sighed and schooled his features into a more charming mask. "Look, I'm sorry."

"But . . . but . . . you and me . . ." Her shoulders hitched up with every word she attempted to say. Hiccups prevented her from continuing. Thank God for small miracles. This situation was painful enough without her having to justify why they were perfect for each other.

No longer interested in Amber's hysterics, Caleb waved one of the waitstaff over. A girl about his age shuffled toward him. He paused.

Her eyes startled him—warm brown with specks of gold. Yet there was no light behind her remarkable irises. It was like she looked past him. Her brown hair fell in a messy braid over her shoulder as if she hadn't bothered running a comb through the strands before weaving them together. Her skin stood out despite the blandness of the country club's uniform of tan slacks and button-down in a color Nathan called sherbet—whatever the hell that was.

This time he didn't bother hiding his grimace when an ear-piercing keen accompanied Amber's hiccups. "Can you bring us two glasses of water?" He glanced at her name tag. "Diana."

Diana Alexander, or Didi as they called her, forced a smile on her face when the stretching of the muscles around her lips was the last thing she wanted to do. She nodded at the trust-fund brat who had reduced the poor girl sitting across from him to a mess of tears, and then turned on her heel to do as she had been asked. She should probably care more, but she couldn't bring herself to do so. If she wanted to make it through this day, she had to keep it together.

At the bar, she took a deep breath that didn't quite make it into her lungs. Exhaling anyway, she concentrated on her task. With practiced movements, she pulled a circular tray from the stack and placed two glasses in the middle. Then she reached for the pitcher with cucumber and lemon slices floating with ice in the rich-people water and poured. Once the glasses were three-quarters of the way full, she balanced the tray on her open palm and returned to the table.

In the background, a middle-aged man asked for extra parmesan cheese. She ignored him, reminding herself to chill. *Just attend to one table at a time.*

She had woken up to a dead alarm clock because the power must have been cut in the middle of the night. This triggered the downhill slide. Her mom had probably run out of money before paying the bill . . . again.

No power meant no hot water, so no shower. To make matters worse, she'd had to make do with yesterday's uniform since she'd been too exhausted to run the wash. And no matter how hard she looked, she couldn't find her white tennis shoes, which forced her to wear boots that had seen better days.

Another patron calling her name surprised Didi out of her head. She tripped as she stepped on the shoelace she kept forgetting to tie, sending the tray lifting out of her hand. She managed to catch the tray by taking a step forward and placing her free hand on the edge. Sadly the two glasses had already spilled their contents onto the blubbering girl with Trust-Fund Boy. The girl screamed and pushed away from the table so fast the back of her chair caught Didi on the hip. This activated a sequence of events that killed her inside. The glasses fell and shattered.

The girl yelled for the manager, then spat obscenities no lady should ever know.

Humiliated and close to tears herself, Didi dropped to the ground and began gathering shards of glass and placing them on the tray. Blubbering Girl wouldn't stop screaming hateful words, adding to Didi's fast-rising stress levels. Doing her best to close off as much of the noise as she could, she concentrated on picking up what was left of her dignity scattered among the glass and lemon slices. She wasn't going to cry. Damn it. She totally wasn't.

When she reached for the largest piece, a hand beat her to it. She looked up into the brightest blue eyes she had ever seen. They were so clear she could almost see her reflection in them. She gasped when the tips of her fingers grazed the back of his hand.

"You don't have to do that," she said quickly, hating how shaky her voice had become. The corners of her eyes stung.

"You shouldn't be doing it either," he replied. "You could cut yourself."

"But it's my job," she insisted, reaching for a clump of cucumbers.

"To cut yourself?"

She pinned him with a withering glare. She'd had just about enough. Her day had to stop getting worse. Or she would explode. Or spiral into a deep, dark pit of despair. Either was bound to happen. She felt it like an itch under her skin.

The corners of his gorgeous eyes crinkled as he whispered, "To be honest, what just happened did me a huge favor." He glanced up and said loud enough for the girl still looming over them to hear, "It's just a little water, Amber. Calm down."

Didi would have laughed if she could have found it in herself to. He had just said the two worst words any guy could say to a clearly distressed female. Something about him being a jerk was yelled. She looked over her shoulder and witnessed pink pumps striding away. She would have breathed a sigh of relief if the stocky form of her manager hadn't been lumbering toward them.

"Mr. Parker, I'm so very sorry," he said.

Trust-Fund Brat stood up. Didi followed him with her eyes, because how could she not? Paying attention, she could make out the best details about him. Besides those eyes, his dark tousled hair was combed to one side. When he smiled at her manager and shook his hand, a hint of a dimple appeared. She was pretty sure the combination of navy sports jacket over a simple T-shirt, and khakis with leather loafers cost more than what she made at the club in an entire year. Add sparkles dancing in the air around him and he would cut a dazzling figure. Hell, it was like he had stepped out of a Ralph Lauren catalogue—all pressed and shiny.

"Don't worry about it, Tony," he said after pulling his hand away from the manager's grip. "Put everything on my tab."

It rubbed Didi the wrong way how he used his money to smooth things over. Sure, she couldn't afford paying for the glasses and the food that had already been ordered, but she didn't need someone like *Mr. Parker* coming to her rescue. Oh, why oh why had he picked her section to sit at today?

Impulsively she pushed to her feet and said, "That won't be necessary."

The corners of his eyes crinkled again. "Really. I'm happy to pay. What's two glasses and lunch? You can even keep the burger and salad." He leaned in, giving her a good whiff of his cologne—cool, clean, and crisp. Expensive. "You saved me. I owe you."

Like water from a burst pipe, words spewed out. "You don't owe me anything. I tripped because I was wearing the wrong shoes. I spilled the water on Ashley—"

"Amber," he corrected.

"Whatever." She huffed. "I'm done! My fault." She yanked off her name tag, threw it at Trust-Fund Brat, and stomped off in the direction of the staff locker room.

The country club sat on a hill overlooking the water. Boats of different sizes tugged against their moorings along the docks, waiting for their owners to take them out. The afternoon sun gleamed, giving the water a shimmer like golden confetti. The sky looked way too clear for the kind of drama Caleb had already been through.

After making sure Amber had left by asking one of the valets out front, he made his way to the limited-edition Mustang his grandmother had given him for his sixteenth birthday, parked in its slot facing the docks. Still in mint condition, it had been his grandfather's car. Given to him by the great Carroll Shelby himself. He would miss the car when he took his gap year, but it was a small price to pay for freedom.

He sat in the driver's seat, not intending to leave. Amber's shrill voice still rang in his ears. Tugging his phone out of his back pocket, he plugged it into the special jack on the dashboard. Then he opened the glove compartment and grabbed a small plastic bag containing a joint and a lighter. He glanced around.

The parking lot looked empty, but considering his luck today, he didn't want to risk adding an arrest for possession with intent to use to his worries.

Slipping the joint and the lighter into his pocket, he left the baggie on the passenger seat and got out of the car. He knew the best place to get high.

Coward's Cliff. It stretched out over the water and was accessible by a path that began at the edge of the parking lot. The stand of trees gave the perfect cover. As kids, he and his friends used to dare one another to jump off. It wasn't too far from the road, but it was secluded enough that a passing cop wouldn't see him from the road.

Caleb ambled down the grassy path, keeping his stride leisurely, hands in his pockets. As far as anyone who saw him was concerned, he was out on an after-lunch stroll, enjoying the rest of the beautiful day. Once he made it to the shelter of the cliff, he fished out the joint and lighter.

Squeezing one end between his lips, he lit the other and inhaled. Holding his breath for a beat, he allowed the magic to work before exhaling in one long, satisfied puff. The smoke curled up in lazy tendrils. He sagged against a tree, tucking the lighter back into his pocket and keeping his hand there. His knuckles brushed against something metallic. The name tag. The waitress. A grin pulled at the corner of his lips.

She'd made him forget himself for a minute. And that was saying something.

He silently thanked her—wherever she might be—for the entertainment and inadvertently saving him from having to face Amber after the tears had dried. Amber would lick her wounds and move on to someone else. There were far richer eligible bachelors for her to latch onto in Dodge Cove. Maybe their breakup this early was a good thing. Now he could concentrate on the trip. Nathan already had most of the itinerary planned out. They had been talking about this trip since he proposed it at the start of the year.

After he'd taken a third hit, a hand snatched away the only thing relaxing him. Caleb straightened as fast as he could under the mellow circumstances. The protest died in his throat.

Pinching the joint between her thumb and index finger, Diana brought it to her lips and sucked in a lungful. Maybe it was the weed working or the shock of her sudden appearance, but he couldn't take his eyes off her mouth. The soft *whoosh* of her exhalation mesmerized him. The way her lips formed an O? Check his pulse, he might have just died.

"Hey," she said in a breathy voice, then took another hit. She still wore the country club's uniform and those ugly boots.

"Hey," he said back, unable to think of anything better until, "Quit hogging my high." Not the best line either. He blamed it on the brain-dulling substance he had been inhaling.

With a huff for a laugh, she handed him back the joint. The idea of returning it to his lips when it had just been on hers made him suddenly very aware of her. The curve of her bottom lip. The upward tilt of her eyes. The long column of her neck. Her citrusy sweet scent.

"Whoa!" He inhaled, eyes wide. "This is some strong shit."

She settled beside him against the tree. Their shoulders touched. "I've had stronger."

"Oh yeah?" came out with an exhale of smoke.

"Yeah." She reached for the joint, and he willingly handed it to her just so he could watch her bring the end to her mouth again.

He thought of something to say and came up with, "Diana."

Her name. Just her name. It sounded so good to his ears for some reason. Yup, his brain wasn't working properly anymore. He reached into his pocket again when she turned her head to face him, the joint still on her lips, and returned the name tag she had thrown at him.

"They call me Didi," she said, running her thumb over her name. "I guess I don't need this anymore."

"Who are 'they'?" He took the joint back, the knuckle of his index finger grazing the corner of her mouth.

She shrugged one shoulder—the one with the braid—then looked out onto the confetti water. "Can you see the future?"

"No. Can you?" He played along, not willing to overthink the sudden bizarre turn in their conversation. He was content to float in her company without actually leaving the ground.

"No matter how hard I look, I just can't see it."

Before he could ask what she meant or anything else about her, the girl they all called Didi pushed off the tree she leaned on, walked up to the cliff's edge, and jumped.

It took a couple of seconds for Caleb's brain to catch up with what had just happened. His heart dropped. Then just as fast, it leapt into his throat. He dropped the joint and toed off his shoes. Removing the jacket, he ran toward the edge and dove in after her, like an Olympian going for gold.

Two

SOMETHING HAD TO give.

The instant she took the leap she felt the pendulum swing up.

Best. Decision. Ever.

She loved the wind rushing against her skin and through her hair. She caught herself thinking this was what flying must feel like. The freedom. The weightlessness. Until *wham*! She slammed feetfirst into the water. The shock took her aback. But there was no stopping now. A grin stretched her lips as her body sank. The coolness banished the stifling heat in her blood. Most people would have fought hard to break through to the surface. She wasn't most people.

Breath left her body in tiny bubbles. The salt water stung her eyes like tears. She struggled to keep them open, blinking often.

What little of the sky she could make out grew farther and farther away.

This must be what oblivion was like. The silence. The cold. Away from hateful words. Hateful stares.

As she sank farther into the darkness, another shape plunged into the water. A shadow she couldn't quite make out until he reached her and wrapped those long fingers around her wrist. Then, with a few quick kicks, her rescuer towed her body from the depths. She wanted to stay under a little longer. Just a little longer. But in seconds her head broke the surface. And as if by instinct, she gulped in the breath her lungs craved.

Two coughs later, an arm wrapped around her front, and soon she was towed back toward shore. Breathing allowed her body to float until her back was almost parallel with the water. She stared up at the sky. Its blue reminded her of the brushstrokes in van Gogh's *The Starry Night*—how the light mixed with the dark until ultimately the dark won, even if technically it was still early afternoon.

Lost in thoughts of swirls of paint, she was surprised when two strong arms dragged her limp body onto one of the docks nearest the cliff. Then she was dropped like a wet towel. An *oof* escaped her lungs, then a giggle.

A face with the most startling blue eyes hovered above hers. No longer were the corners crinkled. Flames burned behind those brilliant irises. She reached up and touched his cheek. His gaze softened slightly. Even wet he was the most handsome boy she had ever seen.

"Wow," she said in an extended exhale, feeling the urge to paint him.

Her handsome boy's expression hardened. "Wow? *Wow?*" He

closed his hands around the collar of her soaked shirt and lifted her. Then he shook her. "Wow? What the hell were you thinking?" He dropped her again, his gaze searching her face.

"My mom always says I don't make the best decisions."

"That part is obvious." He wiped his hand over his still-dripping face. A deep sadness replaced the anger in his eyes. "Whatever you've got going on isn't worth killing yourself over."

"Who says I wanted to kill myself?"

"Uh, maybe the fact that you walked to the edge and didn't stop until you went over? That shows intent."

"No intent. Just what I needed. It felt damn good." She whooped, then laughed up at the crystalline sky. Then she paused, remembering. "I still don't know your name other than 'Trust-Fund Boy' or Mr. Parker. I would like a chance to thank my hero properly. Not that I needed saving, mind you."

His face was so expressive. It was fun watching all the emotions flit across his features. The brow-crinkling doubt. The eye-tightening anger. And most of all, the slack-jawed shock. He closed his mouth and a muscle ticked along his strong jaw. Didi reached up again and traced the line from his ear to his chin with her fingertip, committing the angle to memory. He sucked in a breath. His wet hair dripped on her face like salty summer rain. When a drop landed on her lower lip, she stuck the tip of her tongue out and tasted it. His eyes widened for the briefest second before he closed them and exhaled. All the tension left his shoulders, causing them to slump toward her.

"Jesus," he said like a prayer. "You're crazy."

She laughed again. "Since the age of eight. So? Your name?"

"Caleb." He flopped onto his back beside her and slung his

arm over his eyes, breathing heavily. He shook his head, rubbing the upper half of his face against his arm. "Fuck. I'm too stoned to think. I don't even know how I managed to rescue you without killing us both."

The way he said it, all serious yet resigned, flushed out the humor in her. "Gee, thanks," she said, annoyed. "I will repeat it as many times as you like. I didn't need saving."

In her periphery, Caleb returned his arm to his side and turned his head so he faced her. "What's your deal? Did some rich guy break your heart or something?"

The *tsk* left her lungs before she could stop it. "Sure, because I seem like the type to jump off a cliff because someone broke my heart."

A beat of silence, then, "Is that why?"

Disbelief at his assumption forced her to face him. Both their cheeks touched the wood, the grain rough against the softness of hers. Inches separated their faces. She felt his breath against her lips. Could he feel hers too?

"I'm not weak. If I was going to kill myself, it wouldn't be because someone broke my heart."

"So you admit to the attempt." His features turned serious again. "What would have happened if I weren't here, huh?"

She rolled her eyes. This was even more absurd than her actual decision to jump. And *he'd* asked her what her deal was? "I'm starting to think you have some sort of unhealthy obsession."

In a flash, he was on top of her, securing her wrists with his hands above her head and trapping her with his weight. That fire she had seen in his eyes earlier reignited. "Didi, promise me, that for whatever reason, you won't do that again."

Her eyebrows met. "You're not making sense."

He sighed. "Attempting to take your life."

"It's called *suicide*."

"Didi," he said between his teeth. "Fuck."

"Do you kiss your mother with that mouth?"

As if she had struck him, Caleb let go of her wrists and returned to his prone position beside her. "My mother's dead."

This time it was Didi who shifted her weight so her face hovered above his. She looked into his eyes and found the pain she had been searching for. "Suicide?"

His nod was so curt she barely noticed it.

Ah, that explained it. No wonder he wasn't willing to let go of the idea that she was trying to off herself. She was about to speak her sympathy for his admission when he reached up and touched her cheek. His hand was so warm against her skin. It took all of her strength not to lean into the touch. Like being in the water, she felt comfort from the contact. He ran his thumb beneath her eye. If she had turned her head slightly her lips would have touched the center of his palm.

"I know we just met," he said. "I know I'm no one in your life, but as a favor to someone who saved your life, please . . . Diana . . . Didi . . ."

She closed her eyes and told herself the shiver running down her spine came from the chill caused by her soaked clothes. Yet in the back of her mind she knew the shiver was because her body reacted to the sound of her name in that smooth, steady voice of his.

"Has anyone ever told you you're demanding after being heroic?"

He chuckled. "You're the first girl I've ever saved, so I wouldn't know." He paused. He liked doing that. "Promise me you'll ask for help instead of taking matters into your own hands. You may not think so, but your life is important not only to you but to those you leave behind."

Having had enough, she moved away from his touch and sat cross-legged beside him. How to put this into words he would understand without giving him backstory? She tilted her head, then said, "Caleb, you were there. I wasn't having the best day. Spilling on your girlfriend—"

"Ex," he interrupted.

"Oh, sorry. The waterworks should have tipped me off. *Ex*," she emphasized. "Soaking her and having her scream at me just drove me over the edge. I lost it." She gave herself a mental high five. People lost it all the time. "Maybe working at the club wasn't the best job for me." She curled her fingers around her ankles and shrugged.

Caleb rose to his elbows. "You're saying you got fired."

"I'd like to think of it as quitting without pay."

What she had been telling him all along finally dawned in his eyes. "So you really weren't trying to kill yourself. . . ."

"*Ding! Ding! Ding!*" She glanced left, then right as if addressing a gathered crowd before she began slow clapping. "By George, I think he's got it."

His lips pursed like he was trying his best not to smile. "You were having a bad day."

"Getting smarter by the minute, ladies and gentlemen." She crossed her arms over her chest and winked.

"I overreacted."

"There's hope for you yet, Caleb Parker."

He threw his head back and laughed. She shook her head and laughed with him. Her day was certainly looking up. This was the most fun she'd had in a while. Maybe there was something to be said about starting the day badly, but if she didn't have another one like it in a long time it would be too soon. Once was more than enough.

A different kind of shiver reminded Didi of her current soaked-kitten situation. If she didn't get home soon, she was sure to catch a summer cold. That would definitely suck.

She pushed up to stand and patted her wet bum as if dusting it off. Caleb watched her in silence, a serious expression on the attractive planes and angles of his face. She definitely needed to paint him. That night. Another reason to go home.

"I can't say it was nice meeting you, Caleb, considering the silly chain of events that led to this stellar first impression I just made." She threw a thumb over her shoulder. "But thanks for the assist back there. I appreciate it."

"So you're admitting I did save you." He wiggled his eyebrows in a creepy, suggestive way that caused her to snort-laugh.

"Rich boys and their hero complexes," she said as she stalked off, not willing to destroy what she considered an already perfect moment.

"Are you seriously going to leave without giving me your number?" he asked. "I say you owe me dinner for saving your life."

When she looked over her shoulder he was still leaning on his elbows, a cocky grin on his face. She blinked, committing the magazine-worthy sight to memory so she could paint it later. "Good-bye, Caleb."

Three

RIDING SHOTGUN IN Nathan's cherry-red roadster, Caleb leaned heavily against the door. With the top down, the afternoon breeze helped ease some of the pounding that had begun between his temples after he'd made the trek back to his car. The pumping beats of "Moves Like Jagger" played in the background. Maroon 5 made his ears bleed, but Nathan was obsessed with Adam Levine, so he tolerated his cousin's abhorrent taste in music as they sped up the winding road that led to the Parker Family Estate.

Breathing in, he said on a sigh, "Thanks for picking me up. I'm too high to drive."

A snort was Nathan's response, in addition to, "And apparently you decided taking a swim fully clothed was a good idea. No more weed for you, buddy."

Caleb slanted a wry glance at his cousin in his green sweater-vest and khakis. Nathan possessed the dark hair and baby blues that came with being a Parker. A devastating combination wasted on the ladies since he had been batting for the other team since grade school. Nathan never hid his sexuality, but Dodge Cove being what it was, most of its residents chose to ignore it, or maybe they were just downright dense. Cases in point: their fathers. Both men kept setting Nathan up with anything in a skirt. Good thing his mother was all for his choices.

"You know I'm pretty much dry, right?" A grin tugged at his lips. "But if this is your way of trying to get me to pay for your car's cleaning, then you don't have to worry. As soon as I get home, I'll make the call."

Instead of taking the bait, Nathan said, "What happened at the country club that inspired your afternoon dip? Weren't you supposed to meet up with Amber today?"

The beginnings of his humor disappeared. So much for some light banter. He had completely forgotten that he'd told Nathan about his lunch plans.

"Amber fell in love with me," he said simply.

"Considering the meat market we live in, you, my dear, are a porterhouse steak. How could she not want a taste?"

"And you're prime rib."

"I see myself more like filet mignon," he replied with a laugh. "And I'm fabulous."

"That you are."

"Don't you forget it."

But when Nathan sighed, Caleb knew he was in for some lecturing. He braced himself by sitting up and resting his elbow on the door frame so he could lean his thrumming temple against his fingertips. Closing his eyes and sending a silent prayer that his buzz would last, he gestured for his cousin to proceed with the flogging.

Instead Nathan said, "Do you want to talk about it?"

His eyebrows rose. "What? Nothing on how I should stop dicking around and find a girl to settle down with?"

"Hell no. We're way too young for that. I say Amber had it coming. You know I never liked her."

Relief came on swift wings. Caleb would have taken a bullet for Nathan. Having him in his corner had saved him from the deep pit of misery the death of his mother had plunged him into that first year. Being an only child, Caleb hadn't had anyone else to count on. At least Nathan had his sister Natasha and their parents. When Caleb's father had traded common sense for defensive walls so impregnable he had no time for his kid, there had been days their fridge had nothing in it but cheese and ketchup. His uncle hadn't hesitated to bring Caleb home like a stray pet after discovering what he was living on.

The twins and their friends had been responsible for keeping him sane. Saying he owed them was an understatement. Nathan and company had come to his rescue so many times he had stopped counting.

"I say good riddance," Nathan added.

"Good to know," Caleb mumbled as his eyes drifted to the rearview mirror, where he could see his Mustang, driven by their friend Preston, following closely.

"Speaking of filet mignon, let's move on to better, more productive topics of conversation."

At this, Caleb sat up, because he knew what that grin on his cousin's face meant. His freedom. If he reached out, he could almost touch it. "I read your e-mail last night. The list of places is growing."

"And that's a bad thing?" Nathan's brow furrowed as he sent a scrutinizing glare Caleb's way. "You asked for a European adventure, and I will give you the best damn European adventure any guy can have. I don't do things half-assed."

"Balls to the wall, and no looking back."

"The continent won't know what hit it. The Parker cousins are on their way."

"I say a week per country and no less."

Nathan tilted his head as if considering it, but Caleb knew better. "I say leave the option of extending to two in case we enjoy ourselves too much. The legal drinking age is eighteen, after all."

Caleb threw his head back and howled. "I like the way you think."

"Shame if you didn't. We start in the UK, landing in London—"

"To say hello to the queen," Caleb interrupted, feeling his excitement from the gut.

Nathan laughed. "That we will. Then we make our way up to Ireland and Scotland and make a U-turn back to London before France. . . ."

Twenty minutes into the trip planning, Nathan drove down the tree-lined driveway of their family estate. The stone monstrosity had been one of the original structures built during Dodge Cove's infancy. The place had history, passed down to the eldest Parker child of every generation. This meant Caleb's father took ownership of the sprawling property with its twenty bedrooms, multiple-function rooms, balconies, terraces, an expansive garden . . . Simply put, if the States had a Palace of Versailles, it would be the Parker Estate. To Caleb, the house was nothing more than a tomb.

Exhausted from all of Nathan's big ideas, Caleb got out of the car and headed straight for the front door. He promised to give his cousin a call in the morning without looking back, while Preston eased the Mustang into the detached garage off to the side of the main building. Caleb needed a nap. Too much had already happened in the span of a handful of hours. He just wanted to sleep everything away and start fresh.

The sound of the front door closing echoed through the house. He didn't move from the black-and-white-tiled foyer with its massive crystal chandelier. It took the staff a week to clean the thing—that was after his father rehired everyone he had fired the first few months after the funeral. Caleb closed his eyes and waited. He ignored the usual sounds of activity the staff made—maids cleaning, the butler puttering about, the gardeners cutting grass—and focused on the sounds his father would make. A barked command or the shuffling of papers or the clomping of expensive shoes on marble. When a minute passed with nothing, hope that his father was spending another late night at the firm blossomed in his chest. He let another minute pass before actually making a run for the curved staircase to the second floor.

He was halfway up when the words "Caleb, get in here!" stopped him.

Tight fists at his sides and shoulders heavy, he cursed under his breath every step of the way to his father's study. Of course the bastard wouldn't have been anywhere else. From the iciness of his tone, it seemed his father wasn't having the best day either. Great. What could the man want?

The door to the home office was ajar. Beyond it he imagined where Jordan Joseph "JJ" Parker, Esq. would be. Probably behind his desk. It was the barrier that had defined their relationship over the years. The hunk of wood had been passed down too, from his father's father all the way back to the first Parker. Caleb had played underneath it while JJ worked, sometimes even falling asleep at the man's feet. Now he hated it with a passion.

"What are you waiting for?" came the stern question from inside.

Squaring his shoulders, Caleb pushed the door open. He only went as far as beyond the threshold. No need to get any closer than he had to. The air crackled with mounting anger. He felt it like static on his skin as he inventoried what could possibly have caused his father's ire.

Despite the windows, the wood paneling lent gloom to the space. The chairs and sofa were all dark masculine leather. Law books covered every shelf. And a twelve-point buck head was mounted above the empty fireplace. The thing never failed to give him the creeps.

"What took you so long?" JJ asked from behind his imposing mahogany desk in a gray three-piece Brioni suit and silver tie, his hair slicked back. Was it too much to ask that he defy Caleb's expectations by standing beside the minibar? Would it be wrong for the man to relax with a glass of the best scotch money could buy once in a while instead of reserving it for his clients?

His gaze drifted to his mother's portrait, which hung on the far wall. Her dark curls fell over one shoulder. The light blue of her gown emphasized the paleness of her skin. An ache settled in his chest. His father had commissioned the painting right after they had gotten married. His mother had been three months pregnant with him at the time. The smile on her face killed Caleb.

But for the painting, the house didn't have any other pictures of her. It was the only clear image in Caleb's mind. With every year that passed, his memories grew fainter, like the eventual fading of a photograph exposed to sunlight. It shamed him that he couldn't even remember the sound of her laugh anymore.

As if reading his mind, his father said, "Margaret was always such a vibrant woman. She had a smile that could light up a room. Every time she entered a space the air grew lighter."

Caleb finally let his gaze take in the man who looked like an older version of himself. He prayed day and night that he wouldn't turn out like the soulless bastard his father was. All he did was work, leaving room for nothing else. If losing someone he loved meant Caleb would have to endure this kind of pain, then he would rather not love at all.

"Father," he said like a curse instead of an acknowledgment.

"I got a call from Richard not an hour ago," JJ said, gaze narrowed.

Amber's father. Shit. Of course daddy's little girl would run straight to him.

"He said you broke his little girl's heart."

"She crossed a line," Caleb said in a clipped tone. "We were just having fun. It was time to move on."

"Margaret would be very disappointed to hear that, were she alive today," came his father's equally clipped reply.

Mention of his mother snapped Caleb's tentative hold on his control. "Like she would be proud of you? That's precious. What would she think if she saw you now?" The instant rage in his father's gaze should have warned him off, but he kept on talking. "Don't you remember what having fun is like?"

"It's time you take responsibility for this 'fun' you're talking about and clean up your act."

Taken aback, Caleb blurted out, "What do you mean?"

"I've allowed you to run wild long enough. Your callous disregard for the feelings of others almost cost me an important client." JJ leaned forward, placing both hands on the damn desk. "You can kiss your gap year good-bye. At the end of summer, you're heading straight to Yale. No more fun and games."

Of all the days for his parental instincts to kick in—when for years his father had been content to neglect him—why now? Dread washed away all of his anger like a cold shower. The tips of his fingers grew damp. "You agreed. You said if I got into Yale and two other universities I could defer admission. Nathan and I already have plans for Europe at the end of the summer."

"Consider all your plans canceled."

"All because I broke up with Amber?" He ran his fingers through his windswept hair, not completely understanding what was going on. Stifling the urge to pace, he locked his knees and stood his ground. "I'm not going to Yale."

"You're going to Yale. Or I'm cutting you off."

Caleb sucked in a breath. Without his father's money he had nothing. He thought fast. There had to be some way of salvaging the situation. Then he realized who he was talking to.

High-powered lawyers were always up for a negotiation. So he said, "There's nothing I can do about Amber, but you have to at least let me make it up to you. Let me earn the gap year back."

JJ pushed away from his desk and moved to stand by one of the floor-to-ceiling windows overlooking the grounds. He stuffed his hands into his pockets, a pensive expression on his face. "You're willing to do anything?"

"Yes," he said without thinking of the possible consequences of his immediate agreement. *Always read the contract before signing*, was what his father used to say. At the moment, Caleb was ready to make a deal with the Devil himself for the return of his precious gap year.

Turning away from the window cast his father in shadow, giving the man a sinister appearance. "All right."

"All right, what?" Caleb asked hesitantly. What exactly had he gotten into?

"For the return of your gap year . . ." JJ lifted a finger for his first condition. "You're taking a summer internship at the firm—"

"But—"

"Do you want this gap year or not?" He interrupted Caleb's interruption.

Backed into a corner, all Caleb could do was nod.

"Good." A predatory glimmer crossed his father's icy gaze. "Along with the internship, I want you to attend all the firm's summer events and be on your best behavior."

Caleb swallowed. His carefree summer spent planning a European adventure slipped through his fingers like sand. "Is that all?" The question tasted bitter on his tongue.

"If I hear even a hint of inappropriate behavior, our deal is off." JJ's features hardened. "Am I making myself clear?"

Biting back a curse, Caleb felt the muscles in his neck strain as he nodded. Then he turned on his heel and walked out of the office.

"Oh, and Caleb," his father called out after him. "You start Monday."

The smugness in JJ's tone frayed his nerves. Something had to be done. He pulled his phone out from his back pocket and dialed Nathan. It took his cousin a couple of rings before picking up.

"Nate," he said into the receiver. "Meet me at the gazebo in half an hour. Bring Preston."

Four

DIDI CLOSED THE front door and leaned heavily against the wood. The silence in the house confirmed what she already knew: Her mother was nowhere on the premises. Probably took another shift at the diner or the grocery store. She hated how much her mother had to work, but after everything that had happened today, her not being home was what Didi needed. The last thing she wanted was to explain herself.

On the walk back from Coward's Cliff, while her socks squished inside her boots, her clothes slowly dried, and her hair frizzed, she thought of Caleb. She imagined him sprawled on the dock, resting on his elbows. The hem of his shirt rode up slightly to reveal an inch of what promised to be a taut stomach. Abs? She hoped so. Beads of water clung to his gorgeous hair. Really, the image was photo-shoot ready. A smile stretched across her lips. She couldn't wait to start painting him.

She had seen her share of good-looking guys while working at the club, but how could she have missed someone like Caleb Parker? He had a face made for canvas. Then she sighed when the reality of her life came crashing back.

Because of him she had lost her job.

No.

Not because of him.

She had lost her job because she let her emotions get the better of her control. Hindsight is twenty-twenty. Nothing she could do now. And it wasn't like she would see Caleb again, so it was a good thing she had left him there on the dock.

A shiver ran down her spine. She hadn't dried completely. First things first, meds. That was the most important item on the long to-do list she had compiled on her walk home. Maybe if she had remembered to take them that morning, she'd still have a job. She reached for the switch by her shoulder and by some miracle the light in the hallway turned on. Hallelujah! Her mother had paid the power bill after all.

She pushed away from the door and pulled off her boots. They fell to their sides with a *thunk*. Leftover seawater streamed from the inside. Her socks followed. She wiggled her toes, savoring the feel of the hardwood beneath her pruned skin.

The door to the second-floor bedroom opened, freezing her on the way to the kitchen. "Didi? That you?"

She didn't have to wait long for Angela Alexander's thin frame to fill the top of the stairs. Her mother had been beautiful once. Before Didi's diagnosis. Now, while she buttoned her store clerk uniform, she looked . . . tired. The lines on her face seemed to deepen with each month that passed. The brown hair she tied in a ponytail was ratty and badly in need of conditioner, maybe even a trim to get rid of the split ends. They had been living on generic shampoo for months. In order to pay the bills and buy meds, her mom juggled multiple jobs, and the stress had taken its toll on her body. A good, strong wind would blow her over.

Guilt sank like a boulder in Didi's stomach. Her job at the country club had helped ease some of the burden her condition put on their family. Without that money, they would have to choose between paying utilities and buying meds. The meds always won out. She sagged against the door again.

"Why are you wet?"

The apprehension in her mother's tone, more so than the question, whipped Didi's head up. Her mother jogged down the stairs and headed straight for her.

"I got fired today," Didi said. No use hiding the truth when she didn't know how long it would take to find another job.

Concern manifested as brackets on each side of her mother's mouth as she asked, "Why weren't you answering your phone?"

Thumping the back of her head against the door, Didi reached into her pocket and retrieved a battered flip phone held together by duct tape. It dripped. "I forgot I had it on me when I jumped off Coward's Cliff."

"What?" Her mother took Didi's face in both hands, searching for the breakdown that usually followed . . . an episode. "You didn't take your meds again. I checked."

Of course she had. She was the one who placed each pill into the daily organizer. The portion marked SATURDAY AM was still full.

"I'm fine, Mom," she said, yet the words sounded hollow to her ears. "There wasn't any power, so the alarm didn't go off, and I woke up late. And no hot water." She sighed again. "Basically everything went downhill from there. I promise I didn't intentionally forget to take my meds. I was just about to take them when you came out of your room."

Why, oh why, of all days had her mother been home? Then she realized that she had left work early. Her shift at the country club wasn't supposed to end for another couple of hours.

As if not believing Didi's explanation, her mother sighed and began rubbing her forehead. "I think you really need to see a therapist. The meds aren't enough."

"No!" Didi caught her mother's wrists in her hands. Those muddy brown irises that used to be so bright stared back at her. "Mom, you know we can't afford weekly therapy sessions. I'm fine. Really."

"You're not fine." She shook her head, eyes flooding. "You jumped off a cliff."

"I just needed to cool off. I accidentally dumped two glasses of water on this rich girl at the club and she started screaming at me. I lost my temper. . . ."

"And lost your job," her mom finished, shoulders slumping.

"Yeah." Didi dropped her arms, letting her hands slap against her thighs. "It was stupid. I was being stupid. I'm sorry. You weren't supposed to see all this."

"D . . ." It came out as a long breath, then a pause. She knew what usually came with the utterance of the first letter of her name. All she had to do was wait. It didn't take long. "You really need to consider attending group sessions. I found one that meets once a week at the community center. Those are free. Please. . . ."

What would group sessions do for her? It was bad enough that she had to go through life without a map, sometimes feeling out of control—like today. She didn't need to share in the misery of others. The meds were enough.

"Mom"—she looked into her mother's eyes without blinking—"I made a mistake. I sacrificed taking my meds so I wouldn't be late and lost my job anyway. You have to trust that I won't make that mistake again."

The same stubbornness Didi possessed straightened her mom to her full height. "We're not done talking about this."

Didi rolled her eyes. "Of course not." She unhooked her mother's purse from the coatrack and slung it over the other woman's shoulder. "If you don't get going, you'll be late. We can't have you fired too."

"Didi," she grumbled. "Don't think I don't know what you're doing."

"How many times do I have to tell you I'm fine?" She waited with bated breath for the response in the game they played after each episode.

It seemed like ages, but finally her mother said with a sad grin, "As many times as it takes." Then she kissed Didi's forehead. "Take your meds."

"Get going."

"And laundry."

Didi opened the door. "Will do a load as soon as I take my meds."

"Dinner—"

"Mom," she said in exasperation, practically pushing the woman out of the house. "Go. I got this."

"I'll check on you later," her mom called back as she hurried down their walkway, passing an overgrown lawn and the car that didn't have gas in the tank. Again.

Mow the lawn. Didi added it to her list as she watched her mother walk toward the bus stop that would take her downtown. Then she closed the door and twisted the lock. The dead bolt sliding into place seemed so loud in the now empty house. She hated that she worried her mother. But what could she do?

Taking a deep breath, she picked up her socks and shuffled to the kitchen. On the table she saw the first note: *Honey, paid the power bill. Love, Mom.* She smiled. Obviously, since the lights were on. At least it was one less thing she had to think about, especially since she had no job to help with the expenses. She turned toward the fridge and found the next note: *D, made lasagna.* The third note was stuck to the microwave: *Already precut the lasagna. Place one of the plates in for a minute.* On top of the microwave was a plastic cover with yet another note: *Make sure to cover the plate or the sauce will splatter. Remember, just sixty seconds.*

Didi shook her head when her eyes landed on the most important note of them all: *Don't forget to take your meds.* It was stuck to the plastic organizer. Mothering from afar, that was what her mother called it. No use delaying the inevitable. She filled a glass from the tap, then opened the PM portion and took out the pills one at a time. Three hundred milligrams of lithium prevented the mania. Twenty milligrams of Prozac treated the depression. Fifty milligrams of trazodone helped her sleep. Klonopin was for her anxiety. And the propranolol was for the shakes. Each one vital. Each one she would take for the rest of her life.

Many viewed mental illness as a weakness. To her it was

like being on a boat alone in the ocean, holding a kite string in one hand and an anchor chain in the other and finding the balance so she wouldn't sink.

With each pill she swallowed, she felt some sort of normalcy return. Of course, the real effects of the drugs wouldn't happen until she digested them, but the mere thought of taking them was enough to calm her down.

Breathing easier, she headed into the laundry room. Opening the washer, she dropped her dripping socks inside and began stripping. When she was in nothing but her underwear, she dumped the rest of the clothes from the basket she had left there the night before and scooped in detergent. With the last of her strength, she turned on the washer, then hobbled the final steps into her room. She fell into bed and dragged the comforter over herself. Painting Caleb could wait.

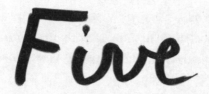

Five

THE FIRST WORDS out of Caleb's mouth as he faced Nathan and Preston across the octagonal gazebo at the far end of the Parker Estate half an hour later were, "JJ Parker has gone insane."

Nathan tilted his head in wonder while Preston . . . well, looked like himself—stoic, with arms crossed. His friend's silence he was used to, but his cousin being unusually mute unnerved him. He had expected a louder reaction than blinking.

He opened his mouth to speak again, when Nathan finally asked, "What the hell happened between the time we dropped you off and now?"

Like a dam breaking, Caleb launched into a fast-paced narration of events. He paced as he spoke, waving his hands in the air.

"Now I have to spend three days a week at the firm starting Monday if I want Europe and the rest of the year off," he finished, breathing heavily. Not five minutes after he had left his father's study, he had gotten a call from JJ's assistant informing him of his duties as an unpaid intern and how many days he was expected to show up at the office downtown. Caleb might not have seen the man's face while on the phone, but the guy sure did sound smug. *Unpaid* had surely been his father's idea, since interns got a weekly stipend when they worked for Parker and Associates. Oh, how far the mighty had fallen in the course of a single day, and he damned Amber to the pits of hell for it.

"So, let me see if I understand everything. . . ." Nathan waved his hand in the air while Caleb concentrated on not hyperventilating. "Because you broke up with Amber, JJ wants you to intern at the firm for the summer and attend all the events to get your gap year back."

Caleb bit back the choice words he had at the mention of Amber's name as Preston added in that deep, quiet voice of his, "Don't forget keeping his nose clean."

"Right." Nathan nodded in his best friend's direction. "Thank you."

Preston crossed his legs, his foot nudging against Nathan's shin. A soft breeze ruffled his sun-kissed blond hair. The muscles in his tanned arms bulged as he gestured toward Caleb. "Is there any chance of you getting back together with Amber until the end of the summer? There are a lot of events sponsored by the firm this year. I already have the invites at home. And knowing JJ, you'll have to attend all of them in order for him to give you the go-ahead to leave for Europe."

"I mean, what's a little over two months of sticking it out

with her compared to the freedom you'll get afterward? Breaking her heart after she successfully shielded you doesn't seem like such a big sacrifice," Nathan chimed in, playing devil's advocate.

"But she broke the rule," Caleb said, a frown creasing his brow.

"Can't you make an exception this one time?" Preston asked.

"No."

Sympathy colored Nathan's tone when he said, "Caleb, you know I will bury a body for you, but sometimes you frustrate me. Love is love. If she feels that way, then let her. It doesn't mean you have to return it. You're already in a bind as it is."

"What does that make me if I string her along for two more months?"

"Someone concerned about self-preservation."

That got him to laugh. "Self-preservation. Right." Then he sobered. "You know Amber. She would want more. More that I'm obviously not willing to give. If I held out until the end of the summer, who knows what would happen?"

Clucking his tongue was Nathan's way of considering things. Preston studied him as Caleb let him work out the logic of his reasoning. It didn't take long for his cousin to catch up. This time when he sighed his shoulders lifted and dropped in resignation.

"You're right. If you string Amber along, her mother will have you two engaged by your birthday party. Which, by the way, will have servers whose sole purpose is to pour champagne."

The excitement in Nathan's tone made Caleb wince. "Can we not?"

"We finally have a theme." He gestured in a wide arc. "The Roaring Twenties. Excess to the max, baby!"

Caleb and Preston shared a groan like animals in great pain.

Nathan's grin was pure excitement. His face practically glowed with it. "We're going to make Baz Luhrmann weep. His movie will have nothing on what I have up my sleeve." Then his expression turned serious. "You know as well as I do that you can't attend those events without a date. The sharks won't leave you alone. It'll be a feeding frenzy."

Matchmaking was the favorite pastime of the Dodge Cove elite. The one percent liked to keep wealth in the family— especially those from old money. Mothball money. If the bank accounts didn't match, then no go. Events turned into meat markets, putting pressure on the unattached to find their soul mates quickly or be forced to endure a merry-go-round of daughters and granddaughters. Not a pretty sight. A lateral move, or even better, a step up were the only viable options. He thought by dating around he would have been immune to this, but it seemed the biddies and mothers didn't care about his reputation. All they cared about was the family he came from and how they could squeeze themselves in.

Using his fingertips, he massaged his temples. "Amber was the last available option."

"What about Cecily?" Nate suggested.

He shook his head. "Sophomore year."

"Tracy?" All it took was for Caleb to shoot daggers at him for Nathan to say, "Oh right, the pregnancy rumors. What a mess that was. Anastasia?"

"Didn't her mother send her to a spa?" He sandwiched the last word in air quotes.

"Then you're screwed. There's no one left our age that you haven't dated and left heartbroken. Many of them are still licking their wounds. The older ones will eat you alive, and the younger ones . . ."

"Let's not go there." He rubbed his face, sudden fatigue eating him from the inside out. "I wish Tash were here. Your sister always knows what to do."

Nathan's lips quirked. "She'd love this. I'm pretty sure she'd tease you into the next century for being a playboy."

"I think her exact word was *manwhore*." He chuckled.

"We could call her," his cousin suggested, taking out his phone.

"And ruin her 'retreat'?"

"You're right." Nathan sighed. "Plus, the last thing we need is to prove to her that we turn into complete idiots when she's gone."

Despite the humor relieving some of his stress, Caleb couldn't help saying, "Why does JJ have to act all fatherly now? He left me alone for so many years."

"Has it occurred to you that this has nothing to do with being a father?" the usually restrained Preston asked bitterly, shocking the cousins into staring at him in surprise.

"What do you mean?" Nathan pressed.

Preston shrugged. "Ever since your mother died, JJ has buried himself in work." He paused, settling those serious green eyes on Caleb. "Amber's father is one of JJ's most important clients. Doesn't he pay your father an absurd retainer?"

"Yeah," he said. "What about it?"

Nathan clapped once, getting Preston's meaning. "You breaking up with Amber threatened JJ's work. That's a deal breaker for him."

Realization dawned on Caleb like a punch in the gut, causing him to stagger onto the opposite bench. "Messing with his work messes with him." He groaned into his hands. "Shit." His gaze darted over the floor of the gazebo as he figured things out. "I bet he knew that by making me attend those events without a girlfriend I would have to fend off unwanted attention. Christ, he's crueler than I thought."

"I hate to say this—"

"Then don't," he interrupted Nathan.

But it was useless because his cousin said it anyway. "You are so screwed."

"Hire someone?" Preston mumbled. He had a faraway look on his face.

"Excuse me?" he asked.

"If you want to avoid a repeat of what happened with Amber and the biddies setting you up with their granddaughters, hire someone to be your girlfriend for the summer."

Nathan threw his head back and howled. He laughed so hard that he hugged himself as if he needed to keep himself from bursting.

Shaking his head, dismay clear in his expression, Preston grabbed Nathan's arm to keep the other guy from falling off the bench.

Caleb rubbed his chin. "A fake girlfriend." He liked the idea.

"And . . ." Nathan sucked in a deep breath, stray chuckles still escaping. "Since you've already cultivated your manwhore image, no one will think twice about you bringing someone new to the parties."

"Gee, thanks." Caleb scowled.

"Happy to help."

"The question is, who?" Preston asked, bringing them back to what they had already discussed earlier.

"I can't think of anyone else." Caleb's hope deflated like a balloon with a small hole. "Maybe Tash knows someone?"

Nathan pursed his lips. "You've already dated all her friends."

"And her friends' friends," Preston added.

"I think I liked it better when you were quiet." Caleb combed his fingers through his hair. He had done that so much today he was afraid he would grow bald if they didn't find a solution soon.

Ignoring the jab, Preston asked no one in particular, "Who do we know that's outside our usual crowd?"

"You want Caleb to contract this out?"

The best friends were arguing the merits of fishing out of their pond, when the image of the girl with startling brown eyes came to mind. Caleb leaned forward, resting his arms on his knees and clasping his hands together. It was a stretch. Aside from knowing her name, she was a complete stranger to him. Would she do it? Who would say yes to attending stuffy parties all summer pretending to be his girlfriend? But she was the only one he knew on the outside. . . .

"I know that look," Nathan said.

"I think I know someone." He bit down on the tips of his thumbs. She had jumped off Coward's Cliff. Maybe she was impulsive enough to agree. But his father had said that he needed to stay on his best behavior. If she was the reckless type, it could become a problem, especially considering the social circles he moved in. "I'm not sure."

"Come on." The whine in his cousin's tone made him look up. "We can't help you if you don't share what you're thinking."

Ah, screw it! If he was to survive, he had to do something. "How well do you know the manager at the club?"

Six

BY FRIDAY OF the following week, Didi had done only three things: eat, sleep, and paint. Not necessarily in that order.

She started by painting his eyes, trying to find the right shade of blue to match how she remembered them. Van Gogh had a thing for blue too. So many shades, so little time. Eventually she moved on to the contours of his face, combining flesh tones like an alchemist in search of the perfect mixture when re-creating the angles and planes. His hair was the toughest part. She had to blend several types of brown, trying to translate onto canvas the right texture of softness she imagined she would have felt if she had given in to combing her fingers through it at the dock that afternoon.

As far as muses went, Caleb Parker was frustrating. She couldn't quite pin him down, and she knew she wouldn't see him again. They might both live in Dodge Cove, but they were galaxies apart.

She was in the final stages of her third attempt when the doorbell rang. With a jolt, she pulled her hand away. Good thing the brush hadn't made contact with the canvas yet, or there would have been a yellow streak across his face.

The bell rang again.

Aside from the occasional pizza delivery, the button beside the front door was hardly ever used. Had her mom forgotten her key or something? Not likely.

When a third ring reverberated through the house, she plunged the brush into the jar of turpentine she kept close and grabbed a filthy rag.

Another ring.

"Coming!" she yelled, rubbing the rag over her fingers to get as much of the paint off as she could. Despite neglecting the cleaning, her mother wouldn't appreciate paint on the door-knob. Which reminded her: *must clean house.*

As a final precaution, she rubbed her hand against her over-alls. Once satisfied she wouldn't leave any oily residue, she turned the lock. Only when the door was already halfway open did she remember her mother's reminder of asking who it was first. *Might be some rapist or home invader,* she would always say.

As a safety precaution, Didi warned in her most threatening voice, "If you're here to rape me or invade my home, I have the nine and the one already dialed!" Then she threw the door wide open. Her lips formed an O when she recognized the person standing on the other side. "You're not a rapist or home invader."

A sexy smile accompanied a raised eyebrow and the removal of aviator sunglasses that revealed those blue eyes she had been dreaming of all week. Damn. They were a darker shade than she had first thought. Or maybe it was because the light was different on her front porch.

"I certainly hope not," he said in a mild tone that quickly shifted to serious. "What kind of neighborhood do you live in that you'd have to ask if you're about to get raped or invaded before opening the door?"

"The kind guys like you don't usually frequent." She took him all in. Blue-striped button-down with sleeves rolled up to his elbows and tucked into mustard . . . "What are those pants called?"

He looked down. "Chinos?"

"I don't know what those are but you pull them off." She crossed her arms and bit the tip of her pinky, enjoying the sight of him. Must have been the confidence in his stance and the way his eyes didn't waver when he returned her assessing gaze. No guys like him at the public school she went to. In fact, guys like him got punched in the face where she went. Well, maybe not Caleb. He looked like he could hold his own in a fight. She'd have to feel for herself to make sure, but from the way the clothes sat content on his frame, she could tell he sported a tight, lean body girls drooled over. Her mouth certainly watered. She wasn't ashamed to admit it. No harm in appreciating God-given beauty. She was a painter; she should know.

"What are you wearing?" he asked.

"My painting clothes," she answered, still admiring him. How could she convince him to pose for her without seeming creepy?

"You paint?"

His tone confused her. "You're surprised?"

"Yes. It's something I didn't expect."

"There are many unexpected things about me."

"I'm starting to realize that."

"Should I even ask how you found me?"

A sheepish grin lifted the corners of his lips. "I asked Tony at the country club."

"Ah." Direct. She liked that about him too. She dropped her arms in favor of tucking her paint-smeared hands into her pockets, hiding the rag as she did so. "Since you're here you should know what my next question will be."

The grin turned into a fuller smile, but no teeth. "I have a proposal for you."

"A proposal?" Her eyebrow twitched. Any normal person would have slammed the door in his perfectly symmetrical face for being so weird. In her case, she found herself intrigued. Why not? It wasn't like she had anything better to do that day besides painting and cleaning.

And job hunting, of course. But honestly, that wasn't going so well. People just weren't hiring. All the summer part-time gigs were taken already. Hence her being home.

"Can we talk inside?" he asked, pushing forward as if expecting her to give way.

She stood firm, barring him entrance. The house needed a general cleaning, and her paintings were drying in the living room. So, hell to the no. Hanging out inside for this proposal of his? Not gonna happen.

Her stomach growled, making the decision for her. She stepped out, forcing him back.

"I figure if you want me to listen to your 'proposal,' you at least owe me lunch," she said, pulling the door closed.

He raked those gorgeous eyes over her body again. He might as well have touched her from the way her skin pebbled from a single look. "Don't you want to change first?" he suggested.

She looked down at her paint-stained overalls and tank top underneath. Even without a bra on she had considered herself pretty much dressed. "What's wrong with what I'm wearing?"

"I believe restaurants have a no flip-flop policy." He pointed at her choice of footwear.

Lifting her foot, she examined the bright pink slipper. "These are my favorite pair too. And here I thought glitter was considered formal wear."

"So you're going to change?"

The hope in his voice made her want to mess with him. "Who said anything about restaurants? I don't have to change for where we're going."

"And where is that?"

With a cheeky grin, she walked past him to . . . Jesus, even his car was gorgeous. White with black racing stripes, the Mustang was all hard lines and lean muscle. Just like its driver. Sometimes money wasn't half bad, she caught herself thinking. Caleb ran past her and opened the passenger door. She paused, eyebrow inching up.

"A gentleman," she said.

He dropped his gaze. Was that pink on the tips of his ears? Her eyes brightened. Oh, he was hiding a blush. She made a mental note to make it a point to unsettle him whenever she got a chance.

Assuming she would get another chance.

"My mother always said it's a man's duty to make a woman happy," he said, locking gazes with her again.

"And you think opening doors will do that?"

"Just get in." There was that equally sexy frown she was growing fond of.

"My, you're pushy." She blew him a kiss before taking a seat. And just as he pushed the door closed, she added, "I like it."

Finding Didi hadn't been difficult. Tony at the country club had been helpful. Well, once he was assaulted by Nathan's potent persuasive powers, anyway. Sometimes his cousin scared the shit out of Caleb.

Even the grunt work he had been given at the firm couldn't stop him from planning out his proposal. How he would approach her about it. How he would broach the subject. He even practiced it in front of a mirror. When that creeped him out, he practiced on Nathan. When Nathan annoyed him by grotesquely imitating someone he hadn't met, he practiced on Preston.

But it still took Caleb days to actually arrive at Didi's door, despite thinking about her nonstop.

A girl taking over his brain like that had never happened before. Maybe desperation did that to a guy. If she didn't say yes, he had no idea what he would do. And now he had her exactly where he wanted her. At a McDonald's. Scratch that. Not exactly where he wanted her. He had originally planned to take her to a family-owned Italian place across town he loved. But men running out of time couldn't be choosers. If Didi wanted a Big Mac with a side of bursting his ego, then she would have it.

He just hoped Nathan would never find out. His cousin

would never get caught dead standing beside, let alone inside, any fast-food establishment. Thinking of the calories would have given him an aneurism.

Feeling out of his element, he watched Didi walk up to the counter as if she had done it countless times before. Speaking quickly, she asked for a No. 1, supersized. The pimply-faced cashier punched in her order and turned to grab a burger in a box, a bucket of fries, and a drink the size of a gasoline can. Caleb blinked several times before he could find the words.

"You're going to eat all that?" he asked, openly staring.

Instead of answering him, Didi said to the guy across from them, "That reminds me, one hot fudge sundae as well, please." Only when the guy turned to get what she had asked for did she look at him. "What do you want?"

He flicked his gaze toward the overhead menu. "Um . . ."

"Don't tell me you've never had fast food before."

His jaw clicked shut. "McDonald's isn't exactly what I call food. If we want burgers, we can grab some at the country club, or choose one of the many other restaurants in town. You sure I can't persuade you to go somewhere else? I know this Italian place. I'm pretty sure they'll let you in." He gestured at her from head to toe.

Nothing seemed to faze her. Instead of frowning at his blatant insult, or worse, throwing some sort of fit like the girls he was used to, she smiled brightly. "Oh, we're totally not leaving now. Not when I know you're a fast-food virgin." He opened his mouth to argue, but she was already ordering the same thing she was having for him.

The next thing he knew he was paying for food that cost less than the gas he had used to drive to her place. Didi shoved the tray into his hands. Trying hard not to spill their liter-sized drinks, all he could do was follow her to a corner booth at the back.

Didi slid onto one bench while he gingerly placed the tray on the table. Then he sat down opposite her, ignoring the way the back of his pants seemed to cling to the bench, and praying whatever he was sitting on didn't stain. He still had a shift at the firm later. Huh. Could he write this off as a working lunch? After all, it did involve a business proposition.

Speaking of business, it was time to get back on track. Caleb tried to remember his carefully rehearsed speech, but he was distracted by what was happening. Didi lifted the stacked burger from its box, took one careful bite, then replaced it into the box. Next she pinched a ketchup packet between her teeth and tore it open. Taking a single fry from the heap, she slid the open corner over the fried potato like she was squeezing toothpaste onto the bristles of a toothbrush. Once a neat red line ran along the fry, she popped the entire thing into her mouth and chewed merrily. After swallowing, she took a sip from her drink and repeated the process over again while Caleb stared, speechless. Burger bite, ketchup on fry, sip of drink, repeat.

"You're not eating," she said after swallowing the sip of soda.

"Has anyone ever told you that you have a deliberate way of eating?"

She tilted her head. He could see the gears inside working. He knew the instant when what he had said clicked. Her eyes narrowed, then widened just as fast. "Oh! You mean the way I eat a burger in a circular pattern?"

For the second time that day Caleb was struck dumb. His

gaze moved to her burger. She had indeed been following the circumference of the thing masquerading as food while eating.

"Why is that?" he blurted out.

Picking up the burger, she said, "The regular way spills all the guts out before you can even finish your food. This way you can enjoy the entire burger without making as big a mess. Plus, they usually place the pickle in the middle. That's my favorite part, so I leave it for last." She put her thumb into her mouth and sucked, ending with an audible *pop* that made him swallow for some reason. She bit into her burger and replaced the still circular mass in its box. Then she covered her mouth while chewing to ask, "So, what's this proposal of yours?"

Seven

FOR A SECOND Caleb doubted his decision to involve Didi in all this. She intrigued him too much. Even the way she ate a fucking burger fascinated him. That was more interest than he had ever given his other girlfriends. Well, granted she would only play his *fake* girlfriend, but it was clear Didi stood out. She didn't fit his usual profile. She was too open, too . . . *real*, for the lack of a better word. His world revolved around the fake—where everyone pretended for the sake of appearances. Could she navigate the tricky social circles? The girls he had been with knew what they were getting into because they grew up attending the same functions and interacting with the same people—*his people*.

He mentally shook his head. No point worrying about things he couldn't change. Breaking up with Amber had backed him into a corner. Which had forced him to fish outside his usual pond. With time running out, he was fresh out of options. Usually he flirted his way to getting what he wanted. Unfortunately he got the distinct feeling Didi wouldn't go for that tactic. So he went with direct.

He let her complete another eating cycle, then leaned in and came out with it. "I need you to pretend to be my girlfriend."

She swallowed her soda wrong and started coughing. When he moved to offer help, she shook her head emphatically at him. Placing a hand on her chest, she rode out the coughing fit by drinking some more.

After a couple more tiny coughs and a hiccup, she managed to squeak out, "I would think a good-looking guy like you wouldn't have problems getting a girlfriend."

He ignored the backhanded compliment. "It's not that simple. I don't need a girlfriend. I just need someone to *pretend* to be my girlfriend. I have events I must attend, and having a date will make things a hundred times easier."

"And why is that?"

Expecting the question, he scanned through his prepared answers. He intended to be honest with Didi. He had no real secrets. If she asked, he would answer.

"Do you know who my father is?" At her slight head shake for no, he thought maybe this was a good thing. Ignorance was bliss, after all. "Simply put, he's a high-profile lawyer. The girl I broke up with at the club is the daughter of one of his most important clients." The words stuck to the roof of his mouth. He had to force himself to keep speaking. "She ran to daddy, and now I'm in this mess. To make up for my mistake, I need to attend all the events sponsored by my father's firm." He left out the internship and the need to stay out of trouble. That information had no connection to what he was asking her to do.

Her eyes narrowed. "And you need a girlfriend because . . ."

He admired the shrewd intelligence behind those burnt-caramel eyes. "Because going alone means I'll be mobbed by matchmaking mothers, aunts, and grandmothers. Not to mention the unattached girls angling to catch my attention. Trust me. It's like blood in the water. The sharks circle. It's been my experience that bringing along a girlfriend—"

"Keeps the sharks away," she interrupted, shaking her head slowly with a disbelieving smile.

Shifting in his seat slightly, he had a sinking feeling she was about to say no. "Something like that."

She snorted. "You are so full of it. But if that's the case, why break up with Ashley?"

The barbs in her tone deflated his ego even more.

"Her name is Amber," he said. "And she broke my number one rule." He waved off the obvious question based on her confused expression. "But that doesn't matter anymore. What matters is I'm here eating junk food with you asking if you would help me . . . just until the end of the summer."

"Then tell me"—she looked straight at him—"why me?"

For asking that question, not with any kind of hostility or suspicion, but with what seemed like genuine curiosity, he respected her more. The answer was simple. "Because you were able to walk away at the dock the other day. That tells me you know your limits. But the real question is: Are you willing to help me?"

The fry she was about to pop into her mouth remained suspended. There went the cogs working again. She had such an honest face. She hid nothing, which might be a problem, considering he was convincing her to step into a world of smoke and mirrors.

Her answer came quick and curt. "Yes."

Disbelief hit him square in the chest. Had she actually just agreed? Then relief followed, but before it could take root she followed up her response with: "Looks to me like this is a lot of trouble to go through for the pleasure of my company at parties."

Smart and perceptive with a hint of spice for flavor. It was a lethal combination that he appreciated more than he cared to admit. His gut told him this was going to be a huge mistake. "I was accepted into Yale."

"Impressive," she said, but her face remained passive.

"And something my father wants."

"Ah." She nodded as if she had reached some conclusion. "You're one of those."

He challenged her by raising an eyebrow. "Enlighten me."

"A Daddy Pleaser." She set down her fry and stuck that maddening thumb into her mouth again and sucked.

"You are so off."

"Really?"

She seemed genuinely interested, so he indulged her. "Going to Yale is the last thing I want." He sighed, rubbing his jaw. "I also got accepted to two other universities, including Loyola. It was part of the deal."

"What deal?"

"Senior year I made a deal with my father that if I got into Yale and at least two other places he would let me take a gap year." The clarity in her eyes told him she was beginning to see the picture he was painting. But just so she understood him properly, he said, "Breaking up with Amber messed with my plans. Now if I don't attend all the events and make nice with everyone, my father will not allow me to defer admission. It's straight to Yale and the life he has mapped out for me."

"And that's your worst nightmare."

"You're getting it. Having you attend the parties with me will make things go smoother. I'll be honest, with the first event looming, you're my only option."

"Burned through your harem of females, huh?"

"Please don't make it sound . . ."

"Misogynistic?"

He hazarded a sip of his own drink to ease the drying of his throat and quickly gave up when the first tablespoon of sugar coated his tongue. "They all agreed to a no-strings-attached relationship. I made sure they understood the rules before we ever started dating."

"And as soon as they broke one you cut them loose."

"No. There's only one rule I'm strict about enforcing."

"And that is?"

In all seriousness, he said, "You cannot fall in love with me."

"Me?" Didi let out a *pfft* sound. "Fall in love with you? Ha! More like the other way around." She pointed at him for emphasis. "Have you ever considered that *you* might fall in love with *me*?"

He leaned back and smiled. "Don't worry. Not going to happen."

She shrugged that maddening one-shoulder shrug. "Don't say I didn't warn you."

Pretending he didn't notice that smug grin of hers, the one

that tempted him to pull her across the table and kiss it away, he kept talking as she returned to her food. "Since we're clear that feelings are off the table, here are a few more ground rules." He tapped the table with a fingertip. "You need to attend all the events with me. This means you'll have to be on call whenever I might need you. Do you have a curfew?"

"No," she said without hesitation. "And since I don't have a job right now, I'm all yours."

Another shred of doubt unsettled him. "You're taking this too casually. Won't your parents mind?"

She thoughtfully munched on a particularly long strip of fry. No potato grew that big. "Why shouldn't I take it casually? My mom juggles jobs like balls and my dad is out of the picture."

"Dead?"

"More like deadbeat asshole."

He grunted at her frank admission.

"It's not like I have anything better to do besides paint. Plus, it's attending parties. Who doesn't like parties?"

Not him. He would rather be sitting by the pool reading and planning his trip, but she didn't have to know that. "They aren't just parties. You need to dress for them. Nothing like what you're wearing now."

"You really have a thing for what I wear, huh?"

For some reason his cheeks burned. "Dressing the part is important. You need to look presentable. That means dresses."

As if insulted, she said, "I have dresses."

"Good." He nodded. "The first event is a garden party, so a summer dress would do."

"When is it?"

"Day after tomorrow. I will pick you up at nine sharp."

"In the morning?"

Her surprise pulled another smile out of him. "Will that be a problem?"

"I'll set my alarm," she grumbled. "What's the next ground rule? How many are there?"

"Not that many, actually. The rest I can tell you as we go. I'm not a control freak." He sat through an adorable eye roll from her, which brought him to one of his main concerns. "You're expected to interact with people. The same people you used to serve at the country club." He paused, letting the silent meaning behind his words sink in. When it did, he continued. "That means no repeat performances of the little outburst you treated me to. No matter how much I enjoyed it."

"You don't have to worry." She pouted. Could this girl get any cuter? He shoved away the possible answers to that question. "That was a onetime thing. I was . . . stressed."

"All right," he said. Something in her shut off, like a candle snuffing out. Where had the vibrant girl unfazed by anything gone? As curious as he was, he reminded himself he wasn't there for that. So he fished out his phone. "What's your cell number so I can text you a day before each event?"

His question brought back some of the life into her eyes. "I don't have one."

"What?" It truly surprised him. "But everyone has a cell phone."

"I don't." She shrugged again. "Well, I did, but it was on me when I decided to go swimming fully clothed. I don't have the cash to replace it."

Unwilling to push further but already making plans, he

returned his phone to his front pocket. "Let's talk compensation. Within reason, of course."

"Compensation?" She tilted her head as if he had lapsed into a foreign language.

"Yes." He inched to the edge of the bench he was sitting on. "I'm prepared to pay you for your time." When she recoiled in horror, he amended, "Didi, besides probably holding your hand or slinging my arm over your shoulder or a kiss on the cheek, I don't expect our relationship to go any further than that. Actually that's another rule. I will not kiss you unless absolutely necessary."

"Define absolutely necessary."

"Most likely in public to prove we're together. Couples kiss, Didi."

"Right." She cleared her throat, then dropped her gaze. "I knew that." A slight flush colored her cheeks.

"I promise I won't kiss you other than when necessary unless you initiate it." He didn't know where those words had come from. That wasn't usually an option he'd verbalized with the others. It had been implied.

She flicked her gaze up. "All right."

His mouth suddenly went dry as he realized he'd just given her permission to kiss him. And furthermore, she had agreed to the possibility.

"So . . ." He swallowed. "Compensation. I was thinking five hundred dollars per event. . . ."

Her eyebrows came together in a scowl. "I take it back."

"Excuse me?"

"I won't go."

"But . . ."

Fire flashed in her eyes. "Don't fling your money at me, Caleb! I'm not that kind of person. Getting to attend the parties would have been more than enough."

"But what I'm asking of you is considerably harder than just attending parties. And it will take time away from your painting and your job hunting. I guess."

That deflated some of her anger. "No big deal. It's just for the summer."

"It doesn't feel right that I'm asking you to do this without me giving you something in return." He considered his options. If she didn't want money . . . "There has to be something you want. Come on, you have to help me out here."

He almost winced at the tiny bit of pathetic that had come out with his last sentence. This was the first time he had ever encountered someone who didn't want something—anything—in exchange for—how should he put it? Services rendered? That sounded so bad.

The sweet blush returned, distracting him from himself. "There might be something."

"What?" His knee bobbed in anticipation as she bit the corner of her lip.

"Will you pose for me?" she asked.

"Pose for you?"

"Yes!" She nodded vigorously. "For a portrait. Please? Please? Please?" She practically bounced off her seat.

Posing for her. Huh. Not so bad. And how could he say no to that kind of excitement? By being his fake girlfriend she was saving him. So why not? This was something he could do for her. "Sure, I'll pose for you."

She clapped, then did the most unexpected thing. She picked up her half-melted sundae and dunked three sticks of fries into the goop and shoved everything into her mouth. As if her eating habits hadn't been weird enough, she moaned, her eyes rolling to the back of her head.

Exactly five seconds later the reality of his situation sank in. He wondered if having a fake girlfriend with him was really better than going stag and hoping for the best. His brain turned off. What the hell had he gotten himself into?

Eight

MANY WOULD KILL for an internship at Parker and Associates. In fact, the rest of the interns had already shunned him for the obvious nepotism involved in his taking the spot from a more worthy candidate—one who had the credentials to match the position, other than sharing the boss's DNA. Not that he had complained. He wasn't there to make friends. Do his time and get out. That was the plan.

Once he punched the button for the fortieth floor and the elevator doors closed, he sent up a brief prayer for strength. He wasn't particularly religious, but after the hijacking of his summer and potential loss of his gap year, he felt the need for divine intervention. God only knew what hideously boring task he would be given today.

In exchange for the morning off, he had to work until the

office closed for the night. Michael, his father's assistant, took great pleasure in giving him the news. If Caleb hadn't known better he'd have thought his father's assistant enjoyed torturing him more than his father did.

At the distinctive *ding* and opening of doors, he was met by said uptight assistant, who wore the most pretentious wire-framed glasses known to man. At least he could appreciate the man's impeccable suit, daring to mix thin pinstripes with a checkered shirt. Nathan would have been proud.

"You're late," Michael sniped, his eyebrow arching. Caleb wouldn't have been surprised to learn the man plucked.

"Lay off, Mike," he said, using the nickname he knew the guy absolutely hated. The way the assistant's entire body clenched was hilarious. "There was an accident on Main. Took forever to get around it."

"He wants to see you," came the clipped reply.

Caleb didn't need to ask who Michael meant. He veered left from the elegantly appointed reception area, with the firm's name emblazoned in bronze letters along the wall behind the receptionist, and headed straight for the largest corner office. The door was open, so he didn't bother knocking as he went in.

"You wanted to see me?"

"Where have you been?" JJ asked without looking up from the file at his desk. He spun a Montblanc pen in his left hand.

"Business lunch," Caleb said, the humor of the idea tickling the back of his throat. He barely suppressed a laugh when his father glanced up in surprise. The pen in his hand dropped and rolled across the page he had been reading. That had gotten his attention.

"Business lunch?" The incredulity in his tone was obvious, yet no real emotion colored the ice in his eyes.

A long pause followed the question.

Feeling generous, he decided to give the old man a break by saying, "I was securing a date for the events you've asked me to attend."

That got him an eyebrow raise so similar to his own that Caleb vowed never to lift his eyebrow again. Matched with a cold gaze, it was disconcerting. "I'm surprised there's still someone in Dodge Cove you haven't dated."

It didn't surprise him that his father knew this. He might not be present in his son's life, but JJ made it a point to stay connected.

Biting back a sigh, Caleb said, "I'm outsourcing the job."

A blank stare was the response to his attempt at a joke. What? Had he actually expected his father, the ice king of DoCo, to crack up? Not in this century.

"Don't bore me with the details." JJ picked up the pen once more. "So long as you are there it doesn't matter to me who you bring." Then he pointed at a large stack of folders. "Make ten copies each and pass them out to everyone involved in the case. Michael has the list."

Before Caleb could open his mouth to confirm the instructions, JJ had already gone back to his reading and pen twirling. Biting down on the sarcasm that would surely get him into trouble, he slid his hands beneath the heavy stack and stalked out.

When he exited the office, Michael slapped the list on top of the stack, then gestured at three more boxes filled with files with a head tilt.

"Those too," he said, not bothering to hide a smirk.

Caleb groaned. At ten copies apiece, that was a lot of dead trees. *Law must be one of the least environmentally friendly professions*, he thought.

As he dropped the folders onto one of the boxes, Michael handed him another list.

"What's this?" he asked, scanning yet another piece of paper.

"Dinner, obviously." Michael sniffed as if he had just been asked a stupid question. "When you're done making copies, you're running out for those. Make sure to check the gluten-free options. Last time you forgot."

He exaggerated the eye roll he gave the assistant. "That was one sandwich."

"Yeah, *my* sandwich."

"Oops?" He had switched out the gluten-free option for something else. How could he have known Michael was allergic to gluten? He thought the guy was just being uppity. Yet he couldn't find it in himself to feel guilty for sending the man home with a severe case of diarrhea and vomiting.

"Just get it right this time."

He gave Michael a mocking salute, then rolled the dolly full of case files to the copy room. In his head he reminded himself to collate. The first time he had made copies no one had told him he had to combine the files in proper order. Oh, the nasty stares and bracing mutters he had gotten from the entire firm then.

Learning his lesson, he had come up with a system. Once he finished the first set and had the second in the machine, he began collating. And staple. Staple. Staple. Lawyers liked their files stapled.

Being alone in the copy room wasn't so bad. He actually found the process quite Zen, the *whir* of the copy machine soothing. He might also be becoming addicted to the smell of toner.

His phone rang midway through. He fished it out and put Nathan on speaker so his hands were kept free. He could multitask with the best of them, but he still needed most of his focus on the job or mistakes would be made. Last thing he wanted was the word *unacceptable* coming out of his father's mouth.

"Yeah?" he said, turning back to the machine as it spit out the next completed file.

"Busy?" Nathan asked back.

The unmistakable *whoosh* of wind from the other end gave him pause. "You're driving."

"I'm using hands-free."

"Still," he insisted. "I'd feel better if you parked before you start talking to me." He ignored the answering grumble and slapped his palm over the stapler, locking the pieces of paper together. Then he slipped them into a waiting folder. Five sets done. Five more to go. He rolled his shoulders to get the kinks out.

"What was that?" Nathan finally asked. No more wind whooshing from his end of the line.

"I'm in the copy room."

"Michael messing with you again?"

"I'm tempted to switch out his order again when I go on the dinner run tonight."

A chuckle preceded the admonition. "Take pity on the guy. He has your father for a boss, after all."

The logic in Nathan's words hit him where it hurt. "Stop messing with my fun."

"Remember, it's just for the summer. Then it's Europe, baby!"

He held on to the thought with white knuckles. He could already smell the London air. Taste the French macarons. Hear Italian being spoken. He breathed in the warm air mixed with the scent of toner in the copy room. "Thanks. I needed that."

"So?" Nathan stretched out the question. Caleb understood from the salacious curiosity in his voice where this was headed. "Did she say yes?"

Nine

FEELING GOOD ABOUT her outfit choice that bright Sunday morning, Didi gave the overall look one last mirror check as the short beeps of a car horn signaled Caleb's arrival. Having chosen to keep her hair down, she flipped the strands over her shoulder and did a quick smile test in case any red lipstick clung to her front teeth. The last thing she wanted was to run out of the house and greet Caleb with a red smear in her mouth. Not attractive at all.

Satisfied and excited to show him what she had come up with for their first event together as a fake couple, she grabbed the cute watermelon clutch she had found at a Goodwill for a dollar from the dresser. Opening it, she placed her house keys, the lipstick she'd used—borrowed from Mom—and a twenty, just in case.

At the third honk, she flitted to the front door with a huge smile and a bounce in her step.

In seconds she was out the front door and locking it behind her. When she turned around her breath caught.

Leaning against the passenger door of his car with his hands in his pockets was Caleb, in an impeccable white linen suit with a butter-yellow shirt opened at the collar. Without product, his hair fell in natural waves—like a dark, wind-tousled halo. He took her breath away, and they both matched: wearing white as if they had discussed it.

Hand to her chest, she checked to see if her heart still worked. Definitely a skip in the beats. She caught herself thinking how lucky she was to have such a mouthwatering fake boyfriend. Oh, this summer had just gotten better . . . until she noticed the scowl that settled on his features.

What the hell was she wearing?

It took all of Caleb's willpower not to smack his forehead. He'd known he shouldn't have trusted her with picking out what to wear for the garden party. A white dress, sure, but she had fucking handprints in places there shouldn't have been. All the blood in his head traveled elsewhere as he pushed away from the car and charged her.

"Caleb?" She took several steps toward him, then stopped once he reached her. "What's wrong?"

"What the hell are you wearing?" he almost roared.

As if she hadn't heard the heat in his tone, she examined the tight thing she called a dress. It had spaghetti straps and an asymmetric hemline that cut so high up one thigh . . . he was no longer thinking with the proper body parts. She had paired it with red canvas flats and a damn watermelon clutch. He breathed out long and hard.

"You don't like it?"

"We are not going clubbing!" He inhaled, but not enough air entered his burning lungs. He might have been having a mild heart attack. "You have handprints covering your breasts."

"Oh, these?" She covered her breasts with her hands to show him. "They're my hands, see? Since I couldn't wear a bra I thought—"

"Stop!" He raised a hand with the word, then shoved shaking fingers through his hair. "I . . . I can't. . . ." He swallowed, then dropped his eyes to the ground. "The grass is the safest place to look right now."

She smiled and grabbed her breasts again, squeezing. "You think I look hot. Is that why you're as red as these handprints?"

"Jesus." He cursed under his breath and took a huge step back. "Please, if you have any shred of mercy, stop touching your breasts."

"Good to know." She laughed. "Let's go. You wouldn't want to be late for this garden party of yours. Daddy dearest might get mad." She headed toward the car.

Running on autopilot, Caleb turned on his heel and overtook her. As he opened the door, he made sure he kept his eyes firmly on the ground. She laughed some more.

"Not funny," he muttered, throat dry. After shutting the door, he hurried to his side and slid into the driver's seat. Then his gaze flicked to her lap. Another curse dropped out of his lips. "Can you please pull your skirt down? I can't be held responsible for crashing this car if you don't."

As if she had taken pity on his obvious discomfort, she

tugged. But, of course, adjusting the hem meant the lowering of the scooped neckline. It exposed the upper curves of her breasts. Caleb gripped the steering wheel so hard the leather made a crunching sound beneath his hands. He couldn't tell if he was the luckiest guy in the world to have a girl like her sitting beside him or if the universe was messing with him.

She hummed, enjoying herself way too much. "Is that your cell phone in your pocket or are you just happy to see me?"

Her question jerked him awake. He reached into his pocket and pulled out the phone he was sure she hadn't really meant to mention. He swiped his thumb over the screen, tapped several times, then brought the receiver to his ear.

A couple of seconds later, the guy at the other end picked up, and Caleb spoke quickly. "I have her." He slanted a glance her way before returning his gaze straight ahead. Yup, looking anywhere else was safest. Not waiting for a reply, he said, "Stay there. I'm driving her over."

In his periphery he noticed her raise an eyebrow.

He hung up and started the car. Over the rumble of the engine, he said to her, "Buckle up, I'm about to break a couple of traffic laws."

Fifteen tense minutes later, during which Caleb didn't speak, didn't even glance her way, Didi leaned half her body out of his car window to get a better view of the massive stone mansion with ivy-covered walls they were driving toward. Gravel crunched beneath the wheels as he skirted a huge fountain that served as a rotunda. She let out an excited hoot.

"Will you get back in here, please?" he begged.

A tugging on the hem of her dress forced her back into her seat. "Is this your house?" she asked, a silly grin on her face. "It's a castle."

Sighing through his nostrils, he said, "This is my cousin's house."

Remembering the call from earlier, she asked, "What's his name?"

"Nathan." Caleb parked the car by the front steps and killed the engine. Even before she could unfasten her seat belt, he was already opening her door. He reached in and helped her out. Heat climbed from where he touched her all the way up her arm, culminating as tingles in her belly.

Needing something to focus on besides how warm his hand was, she let go and yanked the stubborn dress down. The stretchy fabric had ridden up her thighs during the drive and subsequent leaning out of the window. When she looked up she locked gazes with a guy who could have easily been Caleb's twin, except with a slimmer build. He walked down the front steps to meet them in white pants and shirt with a seersucker blazer on top.

"Jesus." He let out a low whistle. "You were right, Caleb. Looking at her is certainly a religious experience."

"Nate," Caleb said with clear warning in his voice.

"Hey." Nathan raised both hands in surrender, "I'm just repeating what you told me about her. Hello." He reached out and took her hand. "I'm Nathan Parker."

His smile was so open and gentle she couldn't help but smile back. Unlike his expressive yet often guarded cousin, Nathan seemed like the type who kept his emotions on the surface. Very much like she did.

"Diana Alexander." She shook his hand. "But they call me Didi."

Nathan and Caleb shared a look before Nathan said, "They?"

Caleb shook his head, then glanced at his watch. "I'm already running late. Can you help her?"

Nathan glared as if Caleb had just stabbed him. "You didn't seriously just ask me that."

"Nate." He gestured toward Didi. "As you can see, I have my hands full with this one."

"Should I be insulted?" she asked Nathan, who granted her another one of those brilliant, almost-all-knowing smiles.

"Don't mind Caleb. He was raised by wolves."

She caught the tail end of Caleb giving his cousin the finger when she glanced at him, and she laughed. She liked them together. The air Nathan carried around him seemed to relax Caleb. They gave her the impression of being close. Being an only child and not knowing what it meant to have family other than her mother, loneliness pinched at her heart.

Must be nice to have a cousin to count on, she thought.

"I have to go," Caleb said, drawing her attention. He was already backing up toward his car.

"I called Preston," Nathan told him. "He's fielding for you with Michael. You're lucky JJ's in court today."

"Just get her there as quick as you can."

"Give me an hour."

Caleb stopped at the driver's side and scowled, sending new waves of shivers through her. For that look alone she didn't mind that he was leaving her with a relative stranger. Emphasis on the word *relative*.

"Thirty minutes," he warned, then got into his car and drove away.

"What does he mean?" she asked the equally handsome boy she stood alone with in the driveway of the biggest house she had ever seen.

"How does a makeover sound?" He took her hand and led her up the steps.

"Is that your way of saying what I'm wearing isn't right for the event?"

"Oh, honey"—he patted her hand—"remind me to sit down with you and give you the basics of thrift store shopping. Will save you a whole bunch of trouble in the future."

"Okay, now that's insulting."

"It's meant to be. Cute clutch, though. We might be able to work with that."

How could she hold on to her building annoyance with the way he smiled at her? Caleb had asked her to attend these events with him. She didn't want to break his rules. If she did, it would mean the end of her summer adventure and the chance of him posing for her. How many girls got the opportunity to enter his world? She had always been curious about how the other half lived, ever since she started working at the club. If he thought what she was wearing didn't suit the event and that Nathan could help, then she would give herself willingly to the experience.

Maybe *willingly* wasn't the right word.

In a stylish bedroom bigger than her house, Nathan sat Didi in front of a vanity mirror bordered with lights. She wondered who the room's occupant could be and wanted desperately to meet her. It was such a beautiful space. One wall was cream with metal wall letters in teal that spelled out LOVE, framed pictures of fun memories and smiling faces hung on another wall, and a third wall had these different-sized mirrors with funky metal frames. But her favorite part had to be the bed. She had never seen one so big, overflowing with throw pillows that had funny quotes on them. She wanted to steal the one that said I'M NOT A LADY BEFORE 10 AM.

She let her gaze wander to the table of the vanity. It was filled with colorful bottles of perfumes, lotions, and makeup. Several different brushes sat in a crystal container at one corner. It reminded her of when she used to watch her mother get dressed for a night out with her dad. Her mom would sit in front of a mirror like the one at which she did now, but with only one light at the top, and begin "putting her face on," as she had called it. A sense of warmth and comfort spread all over Didi at the memory from a time when everything in her life seemed perfect.

For the last five minutes Nathan had been staring at her reflection and running his fingers through her hair. Nerves bundled in her stomach. She was having reservations about the experience already, and they hadn't even done anything yet.

"Um . . . Nathan," she said when the silence got too intense.

"I'm about to become very intimate with your hair. I think that's earned you the right to call me Nate." He took the ends of the limp strands and examined them with a thoughtful frown. "What have you been using for shampoo? Detergent?"

"I just use whatever's in the bathroom. Usually the latest

no-name brand my mom brings home for five dollars a gallon." She chuckled at Nate's absolute horror. "Poor-people problems."

He clucked his tongue. "I cannot have you walking into that party with hair stiffer than a broom." He picked up a pair of slim silver scissors and *snipped, snipped* at the air.

She flinched at the sound the blades rubbing together made. "I'm suddenly not so sure about this."

Nathan leaned down until they were at face level in the mirror together. "You're in good hands, I promise. If only we had time I would have brought you to my sister's stylist. Reynaldo is simply the best. But since we're pressed for time, I'll have to do."

She swallowed and nodded before closing her eyes.

Five inches of hair later, she stared at her reflection as if she were looking at a different person. Nate had given her a messy bob that floated just above her shoulders. Her hair actually framed her face instead of just hanging lifeless around her head. "Wow!"

"Oh, honey, you haven't seen anything yet." He handed her a wet wipe he had tugged out of a plastic container. "Clean off that ridiculous caked-on makeup. Your face is not a wall that needs plastering. Then pay attention. What I will teach you will last you from day to night for the rest of the summer. Maybe even for the rest of your life."

She nodded dumbly. No one had ever taken the time to teach her anything about primping. She learned by copying the girls at school. If Nathan could make her hair look awesome by chopping off the length, then surely he could transform her face just the same.

In minutes, like watching a fast-forwarded video tutorial,

he did indeed transform her face. He applied foundation with a deft touch. He curled her eyelashes and swiped on mascara like a magician waving a wand. He used eye shadow and blush brushes the way she did paintbrushes. One after the other, Nathan applied makeup without any hesitation in his movements.

They had already passed the half-hour mark Caleb had set for her makeover when Nate led her into a huge closet found at the far side of the bedroom. Her eyes practically popped out of her skull when she took in the entire space.

"You have your own mall?" She stepped in without touching anything. All the racks were color-coordinated and organized. Skirts on one bar, dresses on another. Blouses on the upper level while pants were directly below. There were even special places for sweaters, coats, and shoes. Oh, the shoes. The soft lighting made everything sparkle.

"No," Nate said in response to her question. He moved toward the summer dresses and sifted through what looked like fifty of them. "But I think Natasha's closet comes close."

She shrank into herself. "Won't she mind me borrowing one of her dresses?"

Nate gave her a look over his shoulder. "Please. At the rate she's going, she won't even notice one missing. Plus, she's currently on vacation, so she's not here to complain. Not that she ever would."

"Is she younger or older?"

He sighed. "Older by two minutes and lording it over me ever since."

"Twins?" She raised her gaze to meet his. Caleb's were a shade darker, but from the way Nate looked at her so seriously in that moment, there was no doubt they were related. "She must be so pretty."

"The prettiest." He turned back around to face the dresses and pulled out a lemon-yellow halter that flared below the waist.

For the longest minute all she could do was stare. It was straight out of the pages of the magazines her mother brought home. She always told Didi that, even if they couldn't afford any of the stuff featured, they could still dream. It was poring over pages and pages of fashion magazines that helped her understand just what kind of dress Nate was lending her. Then she stepped forward and took the skirt of the garment in her hands. The fabric was soft; it had weight to it without sacrificing movement. With her height, the length would come just below the knee.

"So this is what fabric made of money looks like," she said in awe.

Nathan laughed. It was a clear and honest sound. "Caleb was right. He has his hands full with you."

"And that's a bad thing?" she asked.

With sincerity that mimicked hers—at least that was what she would have liked to believe—he shook his head. "I think he'll enjoy the challenge. We may have just met, but I'm on your side, honey."

"I think I knew that the moment you chopped off my hair."

His toothy grin returned. "If I didn't enjoy pecs more than breasts, I honestly would give Caleb a run for his money."

"You're gay?" she teased, giving him a mock eyebrow lift that he mirrored.

"What gave it away?" He brought the dress to his chin and twirled around with it.

She laughed a full belly laugh. "Do you think that will fit me?"

He winked at her. "Oh, honey, nothing a stick of butter and a roll of plastic wrap can't fix."

Ten

AFTER CHECKING IN with Michael, who gave him strict instructions from JJ to mingle, Caleb decided to head for the biddies. He figured they were the safest group to hang around while waiting for Nathan to arrive with his fake girlfriend, hopefully made over into a brand-new Didi on the outside. Knowing his cousin's considerable talents, he was confident she would fit right in with the DoCo elite once Nathan was done with her.

Unfortunately, on his way to the gaggle of the richest matriarchs, he was intercepted by one of the mothers. She pushed a plate into his hands that contained the customary array of hors d'oeuvres with a side order of a not-so-subtle mention that her daughter was single.

Jesus. Sharks. It was like they scented him and every unattached male within the party's perimeter.

As soon as he had politely declined the mother's offering of a bride and entered the garden, he had been invited to no less than ten events outside the ones he already had to attend for the firm—several birthday parties, dinners, and a slew of Fourth of July brunches, barbecues, and soirees—some of which were scheduled on the same day.

It took him a good thirty minutes to make it to the relative safety of Mrs. Hassleback's group. She was the widow of an oil tycoon responsible for several pipelines running through Alaska, and her ever-present choker of pearls bobbed as she regaled everyone with how her prized stallion had acquired his latest blue ribbon. Mind-numbing, but the mothers didn't dare interrupt the biddies when they gathered, so he endured. His brain imploded the moment the conversation segued into stud services because, of course, this came back around to him being available for their granddaughters, who were somewhere, and if he could wait just a moment they would be summoned. It sickened him that they—the eligibles—were all seen as broodmares and stud stallions until they were paired off in the name of "love." Blah.

Checking his watch for what seemed like the hundredth time, he cursed his cousin for being late and leaving him to fend for himself. Normally he would have been by Preston's side, but the swimmer from the Grant clan was just as much of a shark magnet as he was. Without Natasha to act as their buffer—there was always safety in numbers—sticking together wasn't in their best interest at these parties.

Where the hell were they?

"Who is that pretty flower with Nathan? Don't tell me he's off the market. My Marcy has eyes for him." Mrs. Hassleback craned her neck toward the carousel ice sculpture by the entrance to the garden. Her cronies followed her line of sight. Murmurs of speculation hummed between all of them.

With his height, Caleb looked over their heads toward his cousin and . . . his throat tightened. There, in a yellow dress that emphasized the elegant line of her shoulders and a new haircut that accentuated the shape of her face, stood the most exquisite girl to have ever graced the Dodge Cove elite with her presence. His expectations had been met and more. Nathan was a miracle worker.

Then ugly jealousy made his jaw tick when Nathan took Didi's hand so she could wrap her arm around his. His cousin was just doing the gentlemanly thing by showing those who noticed that Didi was off limits. But damn if it wasn't his role to do that.

Clearing his throat to catch the attention of Mrs. Hassleback and company, he said with pride and something else he dared not investigate right then, "That's Diana Alexander. My girlfriend."

"Well," Mrs. Hassleback exhaled, hand to her rather large rack.

"If you will excuse me." He treated them all to a cordial smile and handed his plate to a passing waiter before easing away from the Chanel-and-mothball-soaked assemblage to head toward Nathan and . . . Didi. Just thinking her name propelled his feet to move faster.

"I should punch you for taking so long," he said when he reached them, but the urge to maim his cousin quickly disappeared the moment Didi looked up at him. Barely-there makeup suited her. Just a soft blush and a light lip. Simplicity at its finest.

"You can't rush perfection," Nathan replied, addressing Caleb's previous hostility. "And from the looks of everyone here and the way your eyes are devouring her, my job is done. Play your role, honey," he said to Didi. "Play it well."

Caleb growled low in his throat, then just to get his cousin back said, "I saw Preston surrounded by debutantes when I arrived."

The air around Nathan sparked. His smile quickly turned into a frown. "If you two will excuse me." He bent down and gave Didi a kiss on the cheek. It took all of Caleb's control not to yank his cousin away when the guy whispered how beautiful she looked into her ear. Didi thanked him with a sweet smile, then focused her gaze on Caleb after Nathan had left. The mischief glinting in those brown orbs drew him in like the moon drew the tide.

"Just so we're clear, you're being hostile toward a guy who will never see me that way." A corner of her lips pulled up. "You get that, right?"

He snorted, then realized what he had been doing. She was there as his shield, nothing more. After mentally telling himself to get a grip, he moved into the space beside her that Nathan had vacated. He took her hand and rested it on his arm. She fit so well against his side he might as well have heard them snapping together into place.

But before he moved her deeper into the party, he gave in to leaning down and whispering, "You do look beautiful."

"See, I don't know if I should be insulted." She pouted. "You left me with Nathan feeling like maybe the outfit I picked out wasn't good enough."

Since the mischief hadn't left her eyes, he suspected she was still teasing him. "Don't get me wrong, I appreciated the previous outfit. Very much." He noticed her skin pebble and ran with the urge to get his own shots in. "But I wanted to save all the lecherous men here from the heart attacks your previous dress would have given them."

In an unexpected move, she pivoted onto her toes and placed a chaste kiss on his cheek. "Then you're forgiven."

For a stunned moment, he didn't know what to do. Clearly she was already in character, right? She was playing the role of his girlfriend. He let the idea settle before using what little brainpower he had left to start moving.

"So this is what a garden party looks like," she said. Her gaze wandered over the sea of light suits and pastel dresses.

Grateful for the topic change, he nodded. "It's just an excuse for people to stand around and talk while the kids play. The men discuss business. . . ."

"While the women gossip," she finished for him. "I can feel their eyes on me. Is that even possible?"

"It's only because you're the shiny new addition to their ranks. They're probably wondering where you came from." He tugged her closer when she had moved away slightly. "And they're assessing if you're competition."

"I'm with you. Of course I'm competition."

The tightening of her hold on his arm did things to him. Things he never thought about with the others he had taken to parties like this. Afraid of what he might find if he dug deeper, he scrambled for something safer to talk about.

"I expected Nathan to put you in heels." He dropped his gaze to her yellow flats.

"Oh, believe me," she said, her voice taking on a breathless quality. "He did. But I've never worn heels before, and I kept tripping. He figured since we would be walking on grass, heels would be my worst enemy. I thanked him over and over again for showing mercy."

"You've never worn heels?" When she shook her head, he followed up his question with "Not even to prom?"

The shrug made an appearance. Light glanced over the top of her exposed shoulder, revealing a shimmer. Nathan must have rubbed some sort of lotion with glitter on her. He had seen the same on Natasha when she wore something that showed a hint of skin. He liked it on Natasha then, but he never knew he would like it this much on Didi. It added an extra sparkle to her that sent a hint of pride spreading through him. Since the Parker princess was absent, he might just be walking around with the most beautiful girl at the party.

"Never been."

Her words sent him back to the present. He eased them into the shade of a tree and leaned against the trunk. Then, by placing his hands on either side of her waist, he positioned her so she was standing facing him. "I find it hard to believe that you've never been to prom. It's a high school tradition."

"No one ever asked me."

Something in his chest twisted at her admission. "You didn't go alone?" The hurt that replaced the mischief in her eyes made him instantly regret his question. "I'm sorry. You're right. I wouldn't have gone alone either." Seeing that he was only digging his grave deeper with each sentence that left his lips, he said, "I love the dress."

Her mood instantly lightened. "Natasha is apparently a size smaller than I am, so Nathan put me in shapewear. Who even owns shapewear?" She huffed, then punched him playfully on the shoulder. "Don't laugh at me. It's not funny!"

Stifling the rest of his chuckles with a fist, he said, "I think that's what Natasha calls 'suffering for fashion.'"

"Yeah, well, no wonder the women at the club only ate leaves. If this keeps up I'll have to live on air and nothing else." She pointed at the buffet table and whined, "Did you see the desserts they have out there?"

"One bite probably won't kill you."

She rubbed her belly. "Don't tempt me."

Taking her hand, he brought the back to his lips and asked, "Remind me again why you agreed to this?"

Didi's eyes twinkled when she smiled. "Caleb, when you came to my house and said you had a proposal for me, not in a million years did I imagine this." She gestured at the expanse of the garden party. "It was like hitting some sort of jackpot. I get to play make-believe with a super-hot guy and at the end of the summer, you leave. Like you said about the others you dated, this is no-strings-attached fun."

"You think I'm hot?" His tone might have been teasing, but inside her words hit him like bullets from a firing squad. If he hadn't been leaning against the tree he would surely be on his knees. But why should her honesty bother him? He wanted this. She would help him navigate this world for a little while longer, and then he would leave. That was their arrangement. If Didi happened to be enjoying herself, then why should it matter to him? It should be a good thing that she took things in stride and went with the flow.

"Correction." She wiggled her eyebrows, pulling his attention back to her stunning face. He made a mental note to thank

Nathan later. He had done a wonderful job. Maybe even too good of a job. "I think you're *super hot*."

"Oh, sorry." He grinned, then placed a kiss on each of her cheeks after he said *super* and *hot*.

She rewarded him with the sweetest blush he had ever seen. Then a scary thought hit him. The summer had barely started and Didi was already holding more of his attention than Amber ever had.

He let go of Didi's hand when he spotted the girl responsible for this mess swaying her hips toward them. "Are you ready to play girlfriend?"

"I thought that's what I've been doing."

"Amber's coming this way."

"Amber?" Didi tilted her head in confusion, then she understood who he meant. "Oh, you mean Ashley."

He rolled his eyes, and she smiled at him before whirling around to face Amber, who had plastered the fakest smile someone could ever give during one of these events on her face—all white teeth and emotionless eyes.

"Caleb," she said in that high-pitched voice of hers. How he had managed to tolerate it all of senior year, he had no idea. "I'm hurt that you didn't even bother to find me and say hello when you arrived. I had to find out from Courtney that you were already here."

Boxing up the annoyance that came with Amber's presence, he returned her smile with one of his own. "Amber, let me introduce you to Diana Alexander."

Didi reached out her hand. "Didi. They all call me Didi."

He held his breath.

When Amber didn't move to take her hand, Didi actually bent

forward and took Amber's hand in both of hers. She shook it vigorously. He swallowed down the laughter fighting to get out as Amber's friendly expression slipped into irritation.

Then Didi slammed things home when she said, "It's so nice to meet you, Ashley. Caleb has been telling me so much about you."

The disgust in Amber's face was priceless. "It's Amber."

"Oh, right." Didi buried herself against his side, forcing him to wrap his arm around her shoulders to accommodate her. Then she patted his chest. "You know Caleb, always mixing up names."

"I didn't know that. Have we met?" Amber's eyes narrowed. "You seem familiar."

"I'm pretty sure we haven't," Didi answered smoothly, never removing her hand from the center of his chest.

Spotting murder in Amber's eyes, he intervened. "I think I just spotted my uncle in the crowd. It's so good to see you again, Amber. Enjoy the party." He maneuvered Didi away from the stewing DoCo socialite. When they were several paces away he gave in to kissing her temple, then whispered, "That was fucking fantastic."

She leaned away so she could look up at him as they ambled through the crowd. "Not regretting this thing between us you started?"

Unsure what she had actually meant, he went with the truth. "After the minor stroke you just gave Amber slash Ashley? Not one bit. You were fantastic."

"I think you mean fucking fantastic."

He threw his head back and laughed before he said, "Come on, let's introduce you to some people."

Eleven

AS CALEB PARKED in front of her house, an overwhelming silence spread between them that Didi didn't quite know the source of. She thought she had played her part well. She even thought she'd done the right thing by pissing off Amber. She had been happy to do it, owing the girl for all the harsh words she had thrown at her the day they'd met. Caleb had seemed okay with it. No admonishments had come from him. She had followed all his rules. Interacted politely. Her smile had come from a genuine place. So why the silence? He had been quiet since they left.

Wringing her hands on her lap, she finally said, "If I did something wrong, tell me so I can improve, change things."

Caleb startled as if realizing she had been sitting beside him this whole time.

"Didi . . ." He whispered her name so softly she almost

wouldn't have caught it if not for the movement of his lips. He took a lock of her hair and twirled it between his fingers. "Did I get a chance to tell you how much I like your hair?"

Resisting the need to run her fingers through the strands, she clasped her hands together. "Why the sudden cold shoulder? I mean, I thought I did okay today. Is it the Ashley thing?" She shifted in her seat so she faced him. His hand fell away from her hair. "Please, you have to tell me. I don't want this to end. I'm having way too much fun. Did you see how Mr. What's His Name . . ." She snapped her fingers. "That bald guy."

He laughed, breaking the uncomfortable tension that had built between them. "You mean Mr. Pritchard?"

"Yeah, him. When we talked about the Impressionists and how I believe the Expressionists were better?" She spoke with her hands, gesturing like she was picking words out of thin air.

Caleb slapped the steering wheel from laughing so hard. "And his face got all splotchy?"

She laughed too, feeling some of the icky tightness in the air ease. "Oh yeah!" She clapped her hands once. "I actually thought he would die on the spot."

"I think he did just a little bit." Breathing hard, he settled heavily against the seat.

"Then why so quiet?" Didi pushed her thumbs together.

Shaking his head, he sighed, then ran his fingers through his hair, further tousling the dark locks. It took all of her self-control not to follow the path of his fingers with her own. In her mind she convinced herself the touch would have been for research purposes. For her painting, so she could accurately capture him. But maybe he had reached his PDA limit for the day. Besides the few minutes with Amber, Caleb hadn't stopped touching her.

"I really feel like I'm not doing enough to help you."

"Hey, you picked me up, gave me a new look courtesy of the fabulous Nathan, and brought me to a party," she said in all seriousness. "I thoroughly enjoyed myself. Especially during that bit where I thought Ashley's head would explode." When he gave her a bland smile, she sucked her lips into her mouth to keep from saying anything else.

Maybe because she was making a funny face, or maybe it was something else, but Caleb's features softened. "I know you said no, but . . ." He reached into the backseat to retrieve a black box and handed it to her. "Here."

She opened it and found a cell phone inside.

"What the hell is the meaning of this?"

"You said yours doesn't work anymore and that you didn't have money for a new one. This one is fully paid for the summer."

She blinked fast to keep the tears from falling. If he had intended to keep her feelings for him nonexistent, he was succeeding. At the moment, she only had room for annoyance. Trust him to ruin a nearly perfect day.

"Growing up, my mom and I only had enough to get by. Sometimes not even that. Once in a while our electric bill goes unpaid, but we manage to survive. I don't know what it means to grow up with money. I can't go out and buy a new phone on a whim, but I've never felt as cheap as you've made me feel just now." She threw the empty box at his head.

He raised his hands just in time to deflect the incoming

missile. The box bounced off the dashboard and landed between them. Exhaling slowly, he thumped the back of his head against his seat.

"Please don't make this an issue, Didi. My number is in the contacts," he said. "The next event is next week. I will text you the details a day before."

She went from frustrated straight to pissed. The tears receded like a well drying up. Not wanting to throw the phone itself at him, she opened the door and stepped out onto the sidewalk. The bastard was getting on her last nerve.

"Didi," he called. "Didi, what the hell?"

Slamming the door, she leaned down and glared at him through the open car window. "Tell Nathan I will have Natasha's dress dry-cleaned and sent back. Thank you for today. I had fun." She said the last word with so much venom, Caleb's mouth actually opened without anything coming out.

Satisfied, she turned on her heel and strode to her house without looking back. When she reached the front door, his car's engine roared to life. The second she stuck the key into the lock he sped away.

Once she was inside the house she went straight to the kitchen and ran smack into her mother in her peach diner uniform. They collided with an *oof*, and she dropped the phone and her watermelon clutch while her mom braced herself against the kitchen table.

"Mom!"

"Didi!" Her mom grabbed her chest, gulping in air. "I didn't expect you to be home."

"Ditto." She bent at the waist and picked up the things she'd dropped. She didn't know what Caleb's deal was, picking a fight with her. There he went throwing his money in her face again. When she straightened, she caught her mother in the middle of giving her a once-over.

"You cut your hair. And where'd you get that gorgeous dress?" Awe and suspicion intermingled in her question. "You didn't buy it, did you?"

"No, Mom. I wouldn't blow money on something this expensive. It's a loaner."

"Did you suddenly find a sugar daddy I don't know about?"

She could tell from the mounting worry in her mother's tone where this conversation was headed. Whatever was left of her anger disappeared. As much as she didn't want to get into this right now, she knew she had to explain before her mom took things to a place Didi didn't want to go.

"A friend at the club invited me to this garden party. I spilled something on my dress so he lent me this. I'm returning it after having it cleaned." She hadn't realized she had been speaking too fast until she noticed the crease on her mother's forehead. "I'm fine," she immediately added. "Taking my meds regularly."

"I know," her mom said, eyeing Didi carefully. "I checked. But suddenly cutting your hair . . ." She hugged herself. "It's nice, don't get me wrong, but . . . are you sleeping regularly?"

"Mom." She turned the word into two long syllables.

"You have to understand where I'm coming from. This is all so sudden."

"I know it looks crazy." Didi waved her hands in the air. "But I'm not being manic. I promise. It's just some summer fun hanging out with a friend. No strings attached."

Her gaze hardened. "There are always strings."

"Not with Caleb," she defended. She might think of him

as a Class A jerk right now, but he didn't deserve to be misunderstood.

A long moment passed where they did nothing but stare into each other's eyes. Didi stayed still, hoping against all hope her mother would see this wasn't an episode. That she knew what she was doing.

"What are the chances you'll do this behind my back anyway if I say no?" her mother finally asked. The seriousness in her tone didn't quite manage to hide her defeat.

"Almost a hundred percent."

"I can't say I'm completely comfortable with this, Didi." Her mother looked her in the eye in the way only mothers could. "But I also don't see what stopping you will do. I know you deserve some fun in your life. God knows I can't give you dresses like that or—"

Didi's hug cut off the rest of what her mother was about to say. "I can't ask for a better mom. Don't think I don't see you worrying over the bills at night when you think I'm asleep."

"Hey . . ." Her mom pushed back so she could cradle Didi's face in both hands. "Do I wish our lives could be easier? Sure. Who doesn't? But don't ever think I'm disappointed that you are my daughter."

"Even if it's keeping you from buying dresses like this one?" Didi joked through a new wave of tears brimming in her eyes.

Her mom kissed her forehead. "Not for all the dresses and shoes in the world."

Twelve

CALEB DROVE AIMLESSLY until the sun turned the sky orange and pink, unwilling to face the emptiness of home while still seething. His frustration finally brought him to the massive man-made lake found at the center of Dodge Cove. Summer homes dotted its surrounding area. He parked his car near the shore and just sat there, staring at the calm water.

He blamed himself for the tears he had seen Didi valiantly keep unshed. All day he had marveled at her beauty and the grace with which she mingled with his people, but nothing compared to the fire in her eyes as she slammed out of his car. He deserved her anger.

He had been so happy with her performance, and then he'd had to go and fuck it all up. At least she hadn't thrown the cell phone itself at him.

He leaned forward until his forehead banged the steering wheel. If she refused to accompany him to the next event, he couldn't blame her. His insides twisted at the thought of the consequences of going stag, but what could he do?

Then the passenger-side door opened, and the car dipped as someone got in. He whipped his head up and lifted his fists, ready to defend himself from the carjacker. A blink later he recognized Preston, dressed in nothing but running shorts and running shoes.

"Jesus, Pres," he said, lowering one fist while raking the fingers of the other through his hair. "You scared the shit out of me. What the hell are you doing here?"

"On a run," Preston deadpanned. "What are *you* doing here?"

Closing his eyes, Caleb said, "I screwed up."

A drawn-out pause followed.

Then, just when the silence between them grew thick, Preston said, "You'll have to specify what you mean."

Laughter bubbled up in Caleb's throat, begging to be let out. Just barely, he managed to keep the humor in, out of respect for the seriousness of his friend's statement.

Without hesitation he described everything that had happened with Didi after he brought her home. He winced at the memory of the box throwing.

"That explains you moping in your car," Preston said.

Others would have taken his words as an attempt at making light of the situation. Caleb knew better. "So, like I said, I screwed up. I wouldn't be surprised if she doesn't want to see me again."

"And you still have several more events to attend for the firm."

"Don't remind me," he groaned.

Another long pause. He let it play out. Preston was thinking, he could feel it from across the front seat. He was at a loss for what to do next. Asking for forgiveness wasn't his strong suit.

"Do you know what she likes?"

The seemingly out-of-left-field question took him aback. "What?"

"Her likes," Preston said. "You must know one thing she's interested in."

The answer popped into his head immediately. "Painting."

"I suggest you drive to the nearest art supply store and fill an entire basket with whatever you think she'd need."

Caleb huffed. "I don't think she'll accept anything from me right now. Might even piss her off more."

"Who says you need to be the one to give it to her?"

Caleb grinned, catching Preston's drift, and started his car. A solid friend was hard to find. "You want to come with me?"

The big guy shook his head, and just as fast as he had come, he stepped out of the car. Without breaking his stride, he resumed his run. Caleb watched his friend's back disappear around a bend, then he put his Mustang in reverse and mentally catalogued all the supplies he had in mind to buy.

Two days later, a red sports car showed up at Didi's house just as she was leaning a painting of the carousel ice sculpture from the garden party against the couch in the living room to dry. She peered out the bay windows to see who had arrived. Her eyes bulged as Nathan slid out of the driver's seat in impeccably pressed mint-green slacks—the kind with the crease in front—and a light gray V-neck. Loafers complemented the relaxed elegance nicely. If Caleb was a Ralph Lauren model,

Nathan easily belonged on some high-fashion runway in his vintage Ray-Bans, which he removed and slid into the pocket of his sweater.

These Parker cousins were gorgeous. She caught herself thinking that if Nathan wasn't gay, she would totally be crushing on him. Then she stopped herself. Even gay she totally crushed on him. Crushed on him hard. A smirk worked its way up her lips.

What was in the water over at Caleb's part of Dodge Cove that produced Adonises? So much hotness in one place should be considered illegal. Or at least made into a tourist attraction. The World's Largest Congregation of Hot Boys. She'd pay to see that.

Her wandering thoughts returned to reality when Nathan produced a large basket laden with what looked like art supplies wrapped in white cellophane topped with a brilliant red bow from the passenger seat. Her heart skipped as he shuffled down her walkway. She scampered to the front door and threw it wide open just as Nathan's finger reached the doorbell.

"What are you doing here?" she asked, breathless in her excitement. Visitors were so few and far between that if she'd had a tail it would surely be wagging.

"Hello to you too," Nathan greeted her, eyebrows lifting.

She turned her attention to the white envelope with her name on it, taped to the cellophane. She slipped out the card and flipped it open. Inside, a masculine scrawl read: *You might want to, but please DON'T throw the basket at Nathan. You'll need the supplies for our modeling session. C.*

Her eyebrow arched. "He sent you to bribe me with gifts? Coward can't even come himself." A part of her was joking, but deep down she couldn't help but feel a prick of disappointment.

"Actually . . ." Nathan shifted the basket in his grip. "He

thought maybe a friendly face would make you more inclined to listen."

"Ah." She stuffed her hands into the pockets of her painting overalls. "So he told you about that, huh?"

"Please forgive him, Didi. He can be an idiot sometimes. God knows, I grew up with him. But in this instance, his heart is in the right place."

When she sighed, her shoulders slumped slightly. "I don't hold on to grudges. I know Caleb meant well. Doesn't mean it was okay."

"At least keep the art supplies. He stayed at the art store until closing putting all this together for you." He lifted the basket as if to prove his point. "As revenge, I say make him pose for you naked."

She tapped her cheek, considering, then a wicked smile spread across her face. "I like this idea. I like it a lot." Remembering her manners, and mentally thanking herself for the general cleaning she had done the day before, she stepped out of the way. "Come inside. Do you want something to drink?"

"Where do you want this?" he asked as he followed in after her.

"Oh . . ." She did a quick scan of the living room. "The coffee table is fine." She indicated the squat table she and her mom had found for ten dollars at a flea market. It was currently cluttered with fashion magazines.

"This is your house?" He set the basket on top of the magazines. The skepticism was unmistakable in his voice.

"Yup," she said simply.

"It's so . . . cozy." Nathan looked around and spotted the carousel painting. "Is this the one from the garden party?"

"Just finished it today." She stood beside her latest masterpiece.

He bent down for a closer look. "You have an eye for detail. The horses are beautifully done."

Stuffing her hands in her pockets again, she rocked on the balls of her feel. "It's still wet so be careful not to get paint on you."

Taking her advice, he moved away from the painting. An almost awkward silence hung between them. Didi waited, but it didn't seem like Nathan had any intention of going anywhere.

"Why do I get the feeling you're not here just to bring over the art supplies?" she finally asked.

"Where's your room?"

"Why do you want to see my room?" A tiny bit of dread fell like a stone in her stomach. The complete seriousness in Nathan's tone made her nervous.

He crossed his arms and gave her the same assessing glance he had treated her to when they first met. "I guess you can say I'm on an exploratory mission." He raised a hand. "Now, before you say anything, I'm here as a friend looking out for your best interest. There are many more events before this summer is over, and Caleb and I had a little talk. . . ."

"You want to see if I have things to wear for all of them," she filled in the blank.

"You're getting it." He smiled. "I just want to save you from a repeat of last time. I don't think Caleb would survive. Will you let me help you, Didi? I promise, I come in peace." He touched the center of his chest with one hand and raised the other as if he was about to recite the Pledge of Allegiance.

All the blood rushed from her face to settle at the pads of

her feet. Compared to his twin's closet, hers might as well be a trash can. "No, thanks. I think I'll shield you from my closet. There are just some things you can't unsee."

Gasping in horror, he asked, "That bad?"

She nodded once.

Nathan closed his eyes for a moment and breathed deeply. When he looked at her again, he lifted his chin. "I think I can handle it."

Admiring his bravery, she sighed and gestured for him to follow her.

"It really can't be that bad, can it?"

"Don't say I didn't warn you."

She could almost hear him pause when she led the way into the kitchen and saved him from having to ask by saying, "Yes, my bedroom is beside the kitchen."

"I wasn't going to say—" The annoyed glance she gave him from over her shoulder cut him off. "All right, so I was going to say something about it."

Laughing, she pushed the door open and led him inside. From her bedspread to her walls, Didi's room was a riot of color. And a complete mess. Never expecting company in there, she hardly bothered picking up after herself. More magazines littered the floor, opened to the editorial spreads that she liked best. At least she had made the bed that morning.

Nathan stopped at the threshold. It was obvious from his expression that he had wanted to hold in the gasp that had escaped his mouth but was unable to stop himself in time. Poor guy looked pale for a second before he steeled himself by squaring his shoulders and marched straight for her closet.

"I call it living in ordered chaos," she teased.

"I like the paint samples on the wall," he said as he pulled open the doors and assessed the clothing inside.

She dropped to her bed and shrugged, letting him do his thing as he pulled out a white crochet dress she had found at the same flea market the couch came from. "They're free. Thought I'd make a collage out of them." And she had. Creating a sort of gradation from light to dark along one side of the wall. It had taken several trips to the hardware store to complete it.

Nathan returned the dress and pulled out another one with a huge picture of a cat on the front. "And where would you wear something like this?"

The shock in his question broke her carefully constructed mask of indifference. She laughed so hard, she almost fell off her bed. She hugged herself and rolled around on the mattress.

"You think this is funny?"

Only the genuine concern behind his annoyance was what made her settle down. "Sorry. Sorry."

He scowled at her before glancing back and dropping the dress he held with a yelp. "Oh God!" He turned away from her closet completely, his face a scrunched-up mess.

"What?" Didi shot up and grabbed his arms, all humor gone. "You didn't see a mouse in there, did you?"

"Worse!" He stared into her eyes. "Polyester."

She dropped her arms to her sides and sighed, shoulders slumping in defeat. This was just ridiculous at this point. "I know you're only trying to help, but I think it's pretty clear that I have nothing in there that will pass. I think I have a fifty lying around somewhere. We can go to the thrift store—"

Nathan shook his head, shooting down the idea faster than

a sniper. "For the events ahead? A thrift store isn't going to cut it."

"Then what?"

"You have to let me shop for you."

"No." She backed away. "Absolutely not."

"Please don't tell me this is about the money."

"Of course it is."

"Honey." He placed his hands on his hips. "I get it. You don't take handouts. But you also need to understand that you committed yourself to helping Caleb. Do you want to let him down?"

That cut her stubbornness in half. "No, of course not."

Nathan took her hands in his, giving them a reassuring squeeze. "Then you need to let me dress you."

"Nate—"

"Please, Didi. It hurts less if you stop struggling. Trust me."

"Rich people." She shook her head in disbelief. A part of her was amused, while the other part knew she would never win so she might as well give in.

Didi led the way into the Greasy Spoon for a late lunch. She kept her hands in her pockets. The shakes had started on the way over. She didn't want Nathan to see. In her mind she figured she was killing two birds with one diner. She would have the chili and introduce her companion to her mother. Hopefully meeting Nathan would go a long way with smoothing things over about the whole summer-with-a-friend thing. Spotting an empty booth, she made a beeline for it and slid onto one of the benches.

"Are you sure about this?" Nathan asked as he slid in after her.

"A little diner food won't kill you," she said, satisfied with her form of revenge. "Be thankful I didn't bring you to McDonald's."

He gasped. "I heard about that as well."

"This must be Caleb." Her mom smiled when she reached their table.

"Mom." Didi beamed, passing the menu she was handed to her personal-shopper-turned-lunch-companion. "I wanted to introduce you to Nathan, Caleb's cousin."

"Hello, Mrs. Alexander," Nathan said, sliding out of the booth and taking her mother's hand. "It's so nice to meet you. Didi neglected to tell me that you worked here."

"I think I know where this is going." Her mother leaned around Nathan and gave Didi a pointed stare. Didi stuck the tip of her tongue out. "My daughter wants to put me at ease with the idea of her being your cousin's date for the summer."

"Please know that we would never put Diana in harm's way. I will make sure that Caleb treats her with respect. My cousin is in your daughter's debt. Thank you for allowing her to assist him."

"I'm not allowing anything," she said. Her eyebrows came together, forming an all-too-familiar crease. Didi thought she had done the wrong thing by bringing Nathan to the diner until her mother sighed. "My daughter does what she wants. My role as a mother is to worry and be there for her when she needs me. I trust she's doing the right thing by helping your cousin. Is he with you today?"

"Caleb is currently at his father's law firm," Nathan said smoothly. "He's a summer intern there. But I could easily give him a call and he can be here in half an hour."

She shook her head and plastered on her server smile. "Let's not take him away from work. I'm sure I'll meet him when the time comes." The last part she said to Didi directly.

"You'll meet him, Mom." She crossed her heart. "I promise."

"Well, then take your seat." Her mother gestured at the booth. "I'll give you a moment to read the menu and will be back to take your orders."

"Thank you, Mrs. Alexander," Nathan said, which sent Didi into a fit of giggles.

When he sat back down, she said, "You look like you were about to keel over."

"Please don't spring a surprise like that on me again," he admonished, rubbing his forehead. "I like to be prepared when meeting the parents."

Her giggles turned into full-on laughter. "Now we're even for backing me into a corner about what to wear for the events."

Thirteen

ON THE DAY of the next event, Caleb showed up at Didi's door with shopping bags in his hands and a delicious frown on his face. Having tucked away all portraits of him into her art room, she stepped aside and let him in. Could anyone say "Here we go again"?

"You're not answering any of my texts," he said, entering the living room and scanning the space.

"Looking for something?" she asked, arms crossed.

"It's so . . . cozy."

She sighed, suspecting the word *cozy* was code for something less polite. "Nathan said the same thing."

He studied the frames on the mantel above the tiny fireplace until his gaze landed on her sunflower painting hanging on the wall. For several minutes, she observed Caleb staring at her work. He looked ridiculous with those shopping bags still in his hands. He looked polished in jeans, a plaid shirt, and boots, but still ridiculous.

"You painted this?" He faced her and tipped his head toward the framed canvas.

"A couple years back. I was totally obsessed with van Gogh. Still am, actually."

"If you hear a voice within you say 'You cannot paint . . . ,' " he said.

Flutters like butterfly wings tickled her belly when she finished, " 'Then by all means paint, and that voice will be silenced.' That's from my favorite quote of his."

"Why aren't you answering my texts?" He faced her fully, expectation in the seriousness of his gaze. "Did you get the art supplies? Nathan said he'd given them to you."

"Thank you for those. And you know I'm totally painting you naked, right? Nathan approves."

He paled. "Please don't tell me you're serious."

"Oh!" She circled a finger over his face. "Just for that look of horror I'm totally making you do it. And you can't back down because that is my price for all this."

"Didi—"

"Wait here." She left him in the living room. Let him stew over her evil plans. The guy deserved to squirm. Entering the kitchen, she veered into her room and snatched the phone from her dresser. When she returned, she found Caleb standing in the exact same spot she had left him. "You actually waited."

His lips twisted. "You said wait. I do know how to follow orders."

Not sure if he'd meant it as a joke, she didn't bother

responding. Instead she handed him the phone. "I never got any texts. I forgot to grab the charger."

Caleb settled the bags on the floor and took the phone from her as his sexy frown returned.

She shrugged. "To be honest, I don't need one. You can have that back. Anyway, like you said, this is only for the summer. That phone is no better than a paperweight after you leave. No one's paying the bill."

He opened his mouth as if to argue. She waited. Closing his mouth and swallowing, he scratched the back of his head and pocketed the phone. "Fine."

"You know where I live anyway. It's not like I've got anywhere else to go." She moved to a pad her mom used for notes hanging on the wall by the front door and scribbled her home number at the bottom, then tore the piece off. "If you really need to reach me, call the landline."

Taking the paper as he had the phone, he stared at the digits for a moment, then snorted. "*Landline*. Haven't heard that word in a while."

"I'm so not getting into another fight with you about being poor," she said.

As if he caught her drift, he picked up the shopping bags and handed them to her. "These are from Nathan. He said you agreed to him shopping for you. Today's event is themed."

She gave him a look. Not like she had been given any other choice in the matter. She suspected Nathan had boa constrictor DNA in his blood. Once you were in his clutches, he would never let go.

"Please don't fight me on this, Didi."

"Since you said *please*."

"Just wear what's in those bags, and let's go."

She would have rolled her eyes at him, but she was too curious about the contents of the bags. Leaving him again in the living room, she hurried back to her room and placed the bags on her bed. She upended the first one.

A rain of brand-new cosmetics and hair products bounced and scattered on her mattress—everything Nathan had taught her how to use for the garden party. Then she peeked inside the second bag.

"Cowboy boots?" she asked loudly, taking out the brown leather boots and blinking at them. When she checked the soles, her size was stamped there along with the words GENUINE LEATHER. She should have known Nate would overspend.

"The event is called the Summer Swing," Caleb replied from the living room.

"You're really going to stay there until I'm done?"

"I think that's for the best, yes."

Shaking her head, she rummaged through the rest of the bag's contents and came up with the cutest pink-checkered linen dress. She had to hand it to Nathan. The guy had taste. Maybe having him as her personal shopper wouldn't be so bad.

"Yee-haw," she said under her breath.

"Did you say something?"

Holding Didi's hand—for appearance's sake, definitely not because he liked how hers fit in his—Caleb led the way to the massive red barn where the Summer Swing was . . . well, in full swing. He hated himself for the pun, but having Didi with him changed the air surrounding them. She lightened his mood significantly after a stressful week at the firm. His father had been on a tear because of an important case. Dare Caleb say he had looked forward to seeing her again? A part of him wished he could have been there when Nathan brought the art supplies. But damn his cousin for even suggesting that he should pose for her naked. Just like him to plant that seed in Didi's head to get him back for making her mad. It had become obvious pretty fast that Nathan was on her side, after he declared her his personal Barbie. The traitor.

And he had met her mother. What must that have been like?

He had come to her house with the specific purpose of picking her up and giving her a piece of his mind for not returning his texts. But as soon as she had opened the door in her painting overalls and dry paintbrushes sticking out of a messy bun, his annoyance deflated. A buoyant kind of happiness had taken its place. He could barely contain himself when she allowed him into her home. Small as it was, the space was warm and lived in, with its comfortable couch, picture frames, and fireplace. And her paintings . . . The vibrant colors went with her vibrant attitude.

On the ride over she had asked him question after question about the event, and he had answered them to the best of his abilities, letting her know that each Summer Swing was different depending on who his father hired to plan it. This particular one they were attending had a Western theme. "Hence the boots," she had said, an impish twinkle in her eyes as she twirled for him after he'd helped her out of the car.

Even from a step behind him, Caleb could sense Didi's barely contained excitement. She squeezed his hand, and he glanced at her from over his shoulder as they walked down the path leading to the barn's entrance. Like Nathan had told him, the pink of the dress—or *rose* as his cousin had called it—set off the paleness of her skin. Her hair, sans paintbrushes, moved as she did, framing a face he had wanted to kiss since she'd come out of her room ready to attend their second event of the summer.

Looking at her was like stepping into a patch of spring sunlight after the harshest winter. Without thinking, he brought the hand he held to his lips and planted a kiss on its back. The move coaxed a gasp out of her. She blushed prettily for him. Just for him.

At the door to the barn, he handed their invitation to a waiting attendant. She nodded them in, not bothering to check the validity of the invite. Didi pulled on his arm, and he slowed his pace and bent down so her mouth came to his ear.

"I knew that face of yours was all the invitation we'd need," she whispered.

The touch of her breath caused heat to climb his neck. He opened his mouth to reply, but Didi was already pulling him forward. The wide space featured a wooden dance floor at the center, stacks of hay bales for seating and makeshift tables, and a sprawling bar spanning one wall. Cowboys moved among the crowd, balancing wooden trays filled with finger food. For those who wanted heartier selections, several checkered-tablecloth-covered tables featured quite a spread of cornbread, an assortment of barbecues, and a bakery's worth of pies.

"Who's that hot piece of cowboy standing with Nathan?" She pointed toward one end of the barn by a stack of hay bales.

A scowl tightened all the muscles in his face as he followed the length of her arm to the direction of her fingertip. Before he could answer, she was already pulling him again. This time toward his cousin.

"Nate, who's your friend?" she asked, not bothering with hellos. Letting go of Caleb's hand and leaving him feeling empty, she shifted her weight to her toes when she stopped in front of Preston. "Your eyes remind me of those old Sprite bottles. I found one at a flea market once. I think it's still lying around somewhere in my room."

Nathan's chuckle caught her attention. "Diana Alexander, let me introduce you to Preston Grant. He's a childhood friend of mine and Caleb's. Pres, this is Didi."

"Can I paint you naked?" she asked, unabashed, looking up at him. Nathan's chuckles became full-blown laughter. She hiked her thumb at Caleb. His scowl deepened. "This one's too shy."

"It's nice to meet you, Didi," Preston said. He seemed unperturbed by her request. The bastard.

She danced to Nathan's side and leaned in conspiratorially, not taking her eyes away from Preston. "Between you and me," she whispered loud enough for Caleb and the object of her fascination to hear, "just how far does his tan go?"

That had done it. The words came out of his mouth without thinking. "If you're going to paint someone naked, it will be me." With impatience running through his veins, he laced their fingers together and tugged. "Come on."

"It was nice meeting you, Preston," she called back, allowing herself to be pulled away.

Caleb gritted his teeth through the shared laughter that followed his retreat.

"There are twinkle lights on the roof beams!" Didi shifted the topic so fast he had to check for whiplash. "And there's line dancing! Can we dance, Caleb? Can we?"

"Yes." He nodded. Her excitement was infectious, making him forget what he had been annoyed about. She had a frenetic energy surrounding her. For the first time since his mother's funeral, he might actually enjoy one of these things. "But we need to make the rounds first. Ready to put your girlfriend face on?"

With mock seriousness, she saluted him. "Yes, sir."

Laughing, he escorted her deeper into the party.

After Didi had navigated the crowd like a pro and played her part with devastating efficiency, Caleb gave Mr. Spencer—an old geezer with more war stories than anyone in Dodge Cove—permission to dance with his girl while he made for the bar with the excuse of needing a drink. *His girl.* The thought had stunned him enough to stammer his order.

The bartender slid a mug of root beer his way as Didi's laughter reached his ears.

"I think it's love," Nathan said when Caleb joined him at the bar.

"What?" he sputtered, spilling some of his root beer.

"Whoa!" Nathan inched away. "These are suede."

He set the glass aside and coughed into his fist. The sweetness of the drink stuck to the walls of his throat. "What did you just say?" he wheezed out.

His cousin returned to his side and gestured with his chin at Didi on the dance floor. Somehow she had managed to take the lead in a line dance. "She's a hit. Half of DoCo society doesn't know what to do with her, and the other half thinks she's charming, according to my sources. Dense and self-absorbed as most of them are, they don't even suspect that she used to serve their food at the club a few weeks ago. Oh, the miracles of a little elbow grease and polish. She cleans up nice, right? And from the looks of things, she paid attention during my makeup and hair lessons. Points for your girl."

His eyebrows came together. "I don't see why her working at the country club would be an issue."

"Of course you wouldn't." Nathan leaned back against the bar on his elbows.

"What does that mean?"

"You're immune to public scrutiny."

Heat climbed his neck again, this time for an entirely different reason. "I'm tempted to dump the rest of my root beer on your suede boots."

Nathan flinched. "Don't you dare! And don't get pissed at me for stating the obvious. It's a good thing Amber isn't here. She's been asking around about Didi. Seems like our ugly-duckling-turned-swan has made quite an impression on your ex."

His rising anger cooled significantly at the mention of Amber. He wondered why she would have any interest in Didi. Then the rest of Nathan's words sank in. "Call Didi ugly one more time and your boots will really get it."

"Now, that's just mean, and after I shared information about Amber too. Unlike you, she doesn't have a father who forces her to attend these things. Whoever decided on a hoe-down for the Summer Swing should be shot."

As if mention of his father conjured him out of thin air, JJ walked into the barn in almost exactly the same attire as Caleb's, except he had a jacket over his plaid shirt and a cowboy hat on his head. Ice replaced the blood in Caleb's veins. Hell had just frozen over.

"What is he doing here?" he blurted out as his father

scanned the gathering right about the same time Didi let out a loud *whoop* on the dance floor.

"I thought he would be in court all day," Nathan said back, in total bewilderment.

"I thought so too." Caleb's stomach sank as his father's gaze finally landed on him. He shifted his weight away from the stool he leaned on to stand straighter when his father began winding his way toward them. Once in a while a group would call for his attention and he would stop.

Tight fists at his side, Caleb flicked glances at Didi. For a crazy second he wanted to pull her out of the barn and escape. Unfortunately for them, his father had already seen him. Leaving would only bring worse consequences later. But he hadn't prepared Didi for meeting JJ Parker. He'd actually hoped they wouldn't have to meet—insane as the thought may have been. Maybe he could make up some excuse. . . .

"Incoming," Nathan whispered before plastering a wide grin on his face. "Uncle JJ, you made it."

"Nathan." His father took his nephew's hand for a brief-yet-firm handshake. "Why did I just get a bill for a fourteen-piece jazz band?"

"Ah." Nathan nodded. "They are the entertainment for the Roaring Twenties party we're throwing our boy. It's going to be spectacular. Trust me."

JJ laughed—full and throaty. "You should have been the one to plan this thing."

"I certainly would have done better than a barn."

JJ laughed again.

Caleb's anxiety rocketed up to the point where pinpricks of sweat gathered along his forehead. His father in a good mood made his actions even more unpredictable. JJ and Nathan spoke about the dreaded birthday party for a few more minutes. When he finally finished with Nathan, JJ moved his attention to his intended target with the efficiency of a predator on the hunt.

"Caleb." He nodded once.

"Father." Caleb returned the nod. The air between them crackled with tension. All the lightness Didi had brought with her evaporated. "I thought you were due in court today."

"The case was dismissed on the grounds of insufficient evidence," he said smoothly. "Since I had time I thought I would drop by and introduce myself to this girl everyone has been talking about."

Caleb's blood ran cold. Shit. Of course news of Didi would have reached JJ. But he never imagined the Devil would actually come to an event just to meet her. He was about to make an excuse when Didi appeared by his side and kissed his cheek before turning her attention to JJ.

"Hello, I'm Diana Alexander." She reached out her hand and kept it there, waiting. "But they call me Didi."

"They?" his father asked in bemusement.

"It's her thing," Nathan clarified.

Fighting the shock brought on by Didi's sudden appearance, Caleb caught the smirk on his father's lips as he took Didi's hand in his. For a murderous second, he wanted to yank her away. She shouldn't be touching someone like JJ. She was too pure. Too good.

"It's nice to finally meet you, Didi," his father said. "I'm Jordan Parker, Caleb's father. You may call me JJ."

In her own innocent way, Didi asked, "What's the other J for?"

"Joseph."

"Okay, JJ." Then she surprised everyone by saying, "I'm still deciding if it's nice to meet you."

In a beat of panic where Caleb scrambled to put out a possible fire by saying something, his father interrupted him by laughing. Again. Was the man drunk or something?

Mute, holding on to Didi's waist, Caleb half-sat on the stool again. He took comfort in the warmth of Didi's hand over his pounding heart.

"Fair enough." JJ tapped the bar and ordered a beer. "So, tell me about yourself, Didi."

And here came the inquisition.

Didi unflinchingly said, "There's not much to tell. I like painting."

"So I've heard. You're an Expressionist?"

"More like a free spirit. I paint what inspiration dictates." She patted Caleb's chest. "In fact, your son agreed to sit for me."

He held in his relief when she left out the naked part. Not sure how JJ would have taken that. He didn't acknowledge the weight in his father's stare, content to keep his eyes on Didi. The way she easily spoke with the cold bastard enthralled him.

"Is that right?" JJ asked. "And your family? What does your father do?"

Didi's signature shrug made an appearance. "I don't know. He left when I was eight."

"And your mother?"

"She has several jobs."

"And college? You do know Caleb is attending Yale."

"Good for Caleb. As for me, I don't know. Maybe I'll attend, maybe I won't. I haven't really decided yet."

"You don't know? You should have made this decision before you graduated. I assume you graduated."

"Unlike you, some of us don't have the luxury of thinking about college."

"Then good luck finding a job without a proper degree."

"What's wrong with making an average living? As long as I get by, I'm good."

"Yes, but besides food, shelter, and basic necessities, you need insurance and money for retirement. Didn't you consider these things when thinking about your future?"

"Well, good thing I can't see the future."

Her unwavering honesty against the disapproving scowl of his father ignited a protectiveness in Caleb he had never experienced before. He was done subjecting Didi to whatever else the lawyer wanted to ask her. She was none of his business. When the music changed to something slower, he interrupted what JJ was about to say by telling Didi, "I believe I still owe you a dance."

The brilliance of Didi's smile undid him completely. Taking his hand in hers, she turned toward the dance floor. He let her lead the way.

"We're not done here, Caleb," his father said, recovering from the blatant insult.

The crowd parted for them. When they reached the center, he placed one of her hands on his shoulder and held the other against his heart. She moved with him willingly, swaying to the pace he had set.

"This is nice," she said. "I've never slow danced with anyone before."

Her admission burned through him. "That's a shame. You are really good at it."

He twirled her around, then pulled her back in one smooth move. She giggled as she settled closer to him, hooking her free hand behind his shoulder. The skirt of her dress brushed against his legs. He nuzzled the top of her head, her hair smelling faintly of turpentine.

"So that's your dad."

"Yeah."

"We didn't talk long, but I get an asshole vibe from him."

Caleb threw his head back and laughed.

Fourteen

EARLY THE NEXT morning, Caleb walked into his father's office with coffee in hand. JJ liked his morning brew black, piping hot, and fresh from the pot. Not even half past eight and already the man was elbow deep in files and scribbling furiously on a yellow legal pad when Caleb placed the cup on the last corner of his desk left uncluttered.

Without looking up from the brief he was putting together, JJ picked up the cup and took a sip.

"Why are you staring at me?" he asked without lifting his gaze from the thick file. "Surely Michael has something better for you to do than stand there all day."

Caleb shifted his weight from his heels to his toes then back again, hands in his pockets. "I guess . . . um . . . I was just . . ."

JJ sighed, dropping the pen on top of his notes. He pinched

the bridge of his nose as he leaned back in his seat. "I did not pay for private school only to have you eat your words when speaking. My time is precious. Either spit it out or leave."

Swallowing, Caleb said, "About what happened with Didi yesterday . . ."

"Didi?" JJ intertwined his fingers, elbows on the armrests. "What about her?"

A kernel of relief sprouted in his gut. "If she overstepped her bounds—"

His father interrupted him by raising a hand. "If this is your attempt at apologizing for the girl, you are failing miserably." Then he lowered his hand and regarded Caleb with that frigid gaze of his. It could have frozen the entire office. "I can't say I approve of her rudeness, but that would make me a hypocrite. My job requires me to be direct when I need to be. She was merely answering my questions. I say that girl has backbone. Certainly more than you are showing me right now. If you think yesterday will affect our agreement, it doesn't."

He held in the breath he had been about to exhale at his father's silent "but" and waited. It didn't take JJ long to continue.

"I understand why you feel the need to bring her to the events. I even understand why you feel the need to flit from one girl to the next—"

"Let me stop you there," Caleb said, finally regaining some of that backbone his father had been talking about. "Don't ever presume to think you understand me. As far as I'm concerned, you checked out as soon as Mother was lowered into the ground. Now, if you don't mind. Michael knows where I am if you need anything."

He left his father's office without looking back.

If loving someone meant becoming like JJ, he would have none of it, thank you very much. He had his cousins and his friends. At the end of the summer he would have a year of freedom. What more could he ask for?

Didi's smile popped into his mind. Unexpected warmth spread across his face when he thought of her. The way she laughed, so light and open. The way the corners of her bright eyes crinkled when she became animated about something she was explaining. Especially anything that had to do with art. And the way she smelled . . . like everything good in the summer.

"Shit!" Caleb jerked as steamy liquid hit his hand.

He had been so caught up in his daydream of her that he missed the cup when pouring the next coffee. Dropping everything, he stormed off toward the bathroom to get cleaned up. He couldn't wait to get on a plane out of there.

About an hour before lunch, Caleb dropped off the latest copies he had been asked to make at Michael's desk. The often surly assistant was on the phone. Michael raised a finger for him to wait. Caleb did so by stepping back and stuffing his hands in his pockets, managing to keep the sarcasm he so wanted to share inside. Then familiar feminine laughter coming from inside his father's office caught his attention.

"Oh, Uncle JJ, what am I to do with you?"

The question drew him forward. That voice. That carefully chosen response. He would have recognized it anywhere. Before he knew it he was entering the lion's den of his own accord, ignoring Michael's protests. His father's visitor wouldn't mind.

JJ looked up from the woman seated on one of the chairs across from his desk and said, "Ah, there you are."

The lightness in his tone didn't deceive Caleb. His father pretended to be amiable for the sake of his favorite niece. But they all knew better.

"How was the south of France?" Caleb asked, pausing a yard away.

The chair's occupant stood and turned. She was a whirlwind of lovely scents and female charm. But pity those who would mistake her ladylike demeanor for weakness. Natasha Parker was the strongest woman he knew. She could deliver a punch like nobody's business.

Her light blue eyes shone at the sight of him. "When Nathan told me that you were interning at JJ's firm I had to come here to see for myself. Is the world ending? Should I be prepared for an asteroid?"

A smirk pulled at his lips. "I missed you too, Tash."

Laughing, she ran into his arms full tilt. He barely had time to brace himself. He wrapped his arms around her waist and lifted her off the ground as she secured hers around his neck. Her giggles filled his ears when he spun them around.

"Caleb, this is my place of work."

In spite of the lightness in JJ's admonition the threat was still there. He returned Natasha to her feet and placed a kiss on her cheek, then stepped back, taking a good look at her. She was much too pale.

"Shouldn't you be a golden-skinned goddess by now?" he asked.

Instead of replying to his question, she looked over her

shoulder at his father and said, "Can I steal him away for lunch, Uncle JJ? Surely he's allowed an hour away from his sentence."

"Consider yourself paroled," his father said, playing along. Then his eyes hardened. "But have him back here in the afternoon. We're prepping for a major case."

Natasha didn't wait for JJ to change his mind. She entwined her fingers with her cousin's and towed him out of the office. He went willingly, taking great satisfaction in the fact that Michael would be left to fetch the lunch orders himself.

Considering their lack of time, Caleb took Natasha to a café a block away from Grant Tower. He was pretty sure JJ expected him back at the firm exactly an hour after they had left. He wouldn't even have been surprised if the man timed it. But he would gladly suffer the consequences for lunch with his favorite cousin.

He pulled back the wicker chair for her at a corner table. She thanked him and picked up the menu sandwiched between the salt and pepper shakers. It was a simple tea shop tastefully decorated with a yellow-and-white color scheme, which he knew Natasha would appreciate.

"What's good here?" she asked as he took his own seat.

"I don't know," he said, glancing at his own menu. "This is my first time here."

She raised an eyebrow, so very much like the way Nathan did. "Figures. This place is way too girly for you. How do you know about it?"

He shrugged. "I pass it on the way to work. It's the closest place that isn't a deli or fast food. I do know how to treat my ladies right."

"Of course. I did teach you."

"And I am forever grateful for your mercy." He touched his chest in mock adoration.

Natasha's reply was to pluck one of the flowers out of the tiny vase in front of them and chuck it at him. He caught it and tucked the stem behind his ear. This garnered another giggle. He had missed her. They all did. Tash being back returned some semblance of order to their world.

"I'm so glad you're back," he said without hesitation. "We regressed to complete cavemen while you were gone."

Natasha lowered her menu and stared straight at him. "I heard you went and got yourself a fake girlfriend." Her eyes widened. "I'm astonished the idea came from Preston, of all places."

"I'm as stunned as you are." He chuckled.

"You have to tell me what she's like."

"Didn't Nathan fill you in? He's been spending time with her too."

"I heard about the white dress she was going to wear to the garden party," she said, folding her hands over her lap. "She sounds like a riot. But I want to hear what *you* think of her."

"There's nothing much to tell." He dropped his gaze, drawing circles over the fleur-de-lis design of the menu. "She's playing her part."

"Yet you can't seem to look at me when you're saying all this. You like her."

His eyes flicked up to catch her grin. "I like her well enough. She's interesting."

"*Interesting*. Is that what you boys are calling it now?"

"Don't go there, Tash."

"If she's able to put that uncomfortable expression on your face I *have* to meet her."

Caleb shifted in his seat. "She'll be at the picnic next week. You can meet her then."

"I think I will." She nodded, then reopened her menu. "Let's eat. I'm starving."

Fifteen

SITTING BENEATH THE shade of a tree on a thick blanket with a pretty rose pattern, Didi brought a grape to her mouth and appreciated its tart sweetness with a moan while she studied the sketch of Caleb she had started. She just wasn't feeling it for some reason, having woken up on the heavier side this morning. She had almost begged off on coming today so she could stay in bed, but she had made a deal.

Noticing that she wasn't in the mood, Caleb had excused her from making the rounds and was off speaking to someone important. She couldn't remember the person's name, even though they had been introduced once before. She didn't dwell since she wouldn't be seeing any of them again after all this anyway.

Not quite getting what she wanted out of the pencil, she flipped to a fresh page and picked up the charcoal stick from her case. A short distance away, Caleb joined a circle of guys she had dubbed the Lacoste models. They all wore polo shirts and a mix between Bermuda shorts and chinos. Would it have killed them to wear jeans outside of a Western-themed party? She rolled her eyes.

Among the group stood Nathan, looking absolutely delicious in red and white. Beside him was Preston in stripes and a light blazer. Both of them together looked lethal—a contrast of dark and light. Her charcoal flew across the white page, quickly filling it up with lines that slowly became figures and forms and faces.

It surprised her that with all the handsome walking around, Dodge Cove didn't have some sort of annual calendar. She bit her knuckle and stared at Caleb, Mr. December. Of all the guys, he was the cool to Nathan's warmth. She imagined him in a gray suit with an ice-blue tie that went with his eyes, and she practically melted on the spot.

"Keep looking at me like that and I'll be forced to kiss you."

She blinked back to the present. Caleb was sprawled by her feet on his side, popping an apple slice into his mouth. How long had she spaced out? She dropped her gaze to the sketch, then at the guys, who were no longer there.

"Well, crap," she said, her shoulders slumping.

Concern on his face, Caleb leaned closer. "What is it?"

She scratched her cheek. "I was sketching you guys and got caught in a daydream. Now you've scattered, and I'm not even close to done."

Shifting up to his knees, Caleb brushed his thumb across her cheek.

"What are you doing?" She would have flinched if her back hadn't been pressed against the tree.

"You have charcoal on your cheek." He chuckled, then tapped the tip of her nose, which made her scrunch it. "There, done." Then he studied her sketch. "That's really good. You got Nathan and Preston smiling at each other just right. Want me to gather everyone again?"

From the earnestness in his tone she knew he would do it too. All she had to do was say the word and he would call the group over to stand at the exact same spot she had been drawing them from. Heart somersaulting, she picked up a grape and pressed it against his lips. He opened his mouth and nipped at her finger playfully when he bit down on the fruit. Heat gathered in her cheeks. As if he couldn't help himself, Caleb leaned forward and pressed a kiss to the corner of her mouth, just missing her lips. He might have promised not to initiate any kissing, but from the wicked look he gave her, he knew what he was doing.

Smirking, she moved to push to her feet with the excuse of being thirsty. Just then, Nathan and Preston ambled over. On Nathan's arm walked the prettiest girl she had ever seen. This gave her pause, staring blatantly.

Wavy dark locks fell past slim shoulders like a sable waterfall. The periwinkle flowers on her dress set off the blue of her eyes. She had a face Renaissance painters would have been falling all over themselves to immortalize on canvas. She was captivating. Then Didi noticed the resemblance between the girl and Nathan.

The trio stopped just outside the blanket.

With a proud grin, Nathan said, "Didi, let me introduce you to my sister, Natasha Parker, princess of Dodge Cove."

Natasha laughed, good-naturedly slapping him on the arm.

Didi got to her feet and curtsied. "It's a pleasure meeting you, Your Highness."

This brought on a round of laugher from the guys as Natasha studied her intently. Then she said to Nathan, "She's everything you said and more, Nate."

"Caleb"—Natasha looked toward him—"I need to borrow your girlfriend for a minute. Do you mind?" Before Caleb could speak, she grabbed Didi's arm and pulled her away from the blanket. "We'll be right back. Girl talk."

All the boys could do was stare wide-eyed after them. A thrill of satisfaction at stumping them washed over her. Didi had never seen someone take complete control of a group the way Natasha had. No wonder the guys worshipped the ground she walked upon.

"Be honest with me," Natasha whispered when they were out of earshot, tightening her grip. "Between just us girls, why did you say yes to being Caleb's fake girlfriend?"

Without hesitation, she said, "Because I had nothing better to do this summer."

The Dodge Cove princess paused in her stride. "Forgive me, but I don't believe you."

"I don't see why it's any of your business."

"I make it my business where Caleb is concerned." Her sparkling blue eyes narrowed, changing her whole face into something scarier. Still beautiful, but definitely scarier. "What do you get out of this?"

Under the weight of that gaze, Didi broke eye contact. She took a deep breath to settle her sudden case of nerves and decided to tell the truth.

"He's pretty. . . . And I thought it would be fun. . . . And it's just for the summer."

There was a pause, then Natasha burst out laughing.

"I think I like you, Diana Alexander." Natasha gave her a kiss on the cheek before she added, "Take care of our boy. He might not look it, but he does have feelings."

"I think I like you too, Natasha Parker, princess of Dodge Cove."

Didi looked back toward their blanket, where Caleb and Nathan were laughing about something while Preston remained his usual statue self. A twinge of envy with a hint of loneliness hit her heart. "And he'll be fine. He has all of you."

A small smile graced Natasha's perfect bow lips. "Why don't you go grab us some drinks while I say hello to Preston's mom. Knowing Mr. Cat Got His Tongue, he probably hasn't told her I'm back in DoCo. Meet you at the blanket."

Nodding, she watched Natasha navigate the crowd like a boss, expertly flitting from one group to another, exchanging pleasantries, until she reached a woman who bore a strong resemblance to Preston. She was gorgeous, like her son, but from the way she stood it seemed like she had a huge stick up her butt. Not someone she wanted to meet anytime soon.

Arriving at the beverage table, Didi contemplated the seemingly endless options. She caught herself muttering "rich people" under her breath. No less than seven kinds of iced teas. Six varieties of soda. Five brands of beer. Four types of lemonade. Three flavors of froufrou water. Two colors of wine. And a punch bowl in a pear tree. She sighed, going for an

Arnold Palmer: half lemonade, half iced tea. Not original, but at least she had satisfied her thirst the way she wanted to.

"You must think this is all too much."

Regretting leaving the safety of Caleb's company, Didi forced her lips into a smile and said through her teeth, "Ashley, so good to see you again."

"Am-ber." She pointed at her purple-sundressed self and carefully enunciated the syllables of her name as if Didi was learning impaired or deaf or both. She totally didn't get it.

Mentally shaking her head and praying for strength, since she thought she had gotten rid of this viper, she went with it. "Of course, Ashley. Didn't see you at the Summer Swing. That was so much fun."

"I don't go to those. Hay." She waved in disgust. "Tacky."

"If I didn't know better I'd think you were allergic." She had meant it to tease her, but from the way Amber stiffened she'd hit the bull's-eye inadvertently. Huh.

She quickly recovered with, "All this must be overwhelming for you."

Crossing her arms brought the cup closer to her chest. "What do you mean?"

Amber sidled closer and whispered, "Must be tough interacting with people who have more . . . class."

Normally Amber's words wouldn't have disturbed her the way they did. "I really don't know what you're talking about."

"Oh, you think I still don't know?" Amber waved again, this time as if she were fanning away a foul smell. "Caleb is just stringing you along. In the end he'll come back to me."

"You're so full of shit. You were a mess of tears at the club."

She realized her mistake as soon as a glint of triumph entered Amber's eyes. "I knew it! You're that waitress who dumped water all over me."

"Not that it's a secret, but yeah. And I'd do it again if it wouldn't embarrass Caleb. So tell everyone. I don't care." Her grip on the cup tightened to the point where the plastic crunched. "It's not going to change what Caleb and I have."

"Oh, of course not." Amber smiled, but steel remained in her eyes. "The people here will just gossip about you. I'm sure words like *gold digger* won't bother you at all, since when this summer is over, Caleb will be gone, and you'll go back to whatever hovel you came from." Before Didi could respond, she added, "But, you see, Caleb's father is a different story. All I have to do is tell him about you—"

"But he already knows about me," she interrupted.

"Not after I add a few juicy details of my own into the mix." The delight in Amber's expression said it all.

Didi had walked into her trap. Whatever the witch had been planning, she'd accomplished, because people were looking their way. Seeing red, Didi shifted to pitch the contents of her cup at Amber's face. But just as her hand tilted toward the girl, who was clearly waiting for it, strong fingers closed around her wrist. In quick movements, she was relieved of the cup and maneuvered behind a fuming Caleb.

"Amber, lower your voice before you embarrass yourself," he said through his teeth, anger radiating off him.

Amber merely tilted her chin up in defiance.

"Whatever it is you think you're doing, it won't change anything," he added in a harsh tone. "Get it into your head. There's never going to be anything between us."

— 133 —

"What do you think your father will say when I tell him about how rude she's being to me?" she hissed.

Squaring his shoulders, Caleb took a step forward. "I'd like to see you try."

"See if I don't."

"Amber," he whispered her name like a curse. "You're forgetting that you agreed to no strings attached with me senior year. Weren't you telling your friends that we were actually going out? That you finally—what was the word you used?" Amber paled, but Caleb continued anyway. "Ah, that's right. That you finally *landed* me? What would your friends think if it got out that our relationship was nothing more than me having a good time?"

"They will believe me over you, of course." But doubt had already crept into her voice.

"Not when they hear the recording of you agreeing to my terms."

"You wouldn't dare!"

"I'd like to think you know me better than that."

Eyes brimming, Amber backed away. Hatred for Caleb oozed out of her like heat from a fire. Her lips twisted as her face settled into a scowl. She must have seen the truth in Caleb's stern expression because she hurried away.

Caleb turned toward Didi and looked her in the eye, all his previous anger turning into concern. "Are you all right, Didi?"

"You didn't really record your conversation with her, did you?" she asked, giving the place where Amber once stood a glance.

"She doesn't know that."

She stepped closer. "You just defended me."

"Actually . . ." Scratching the back of his head, he grinned. "I was saving Amber from your wrath. I have money on you winning, but I don't think everyone is ready for a UFC cage match to play out. There are kids present, after all."

"You don't think she'll actually tell your father, do you?"

Caleb stroked his knuckles down her cheek. "Let me worry about that."

"But your dad—"

"Won't be a problem. Trust me."

A hum of appreciation escaped her throat. "You don't know how unbelievably hot it is that you think I'd win against Ashley."

"Oh yeah?" He circled her waist with his arms, pulling her closer.

"Yeah." She shifted onto her toes and kissed his cheek. Then before he could respond, she pushed back and said, "Tomorrow, my house."

"Your house," he repeated. Desire ignited in his gaze, turning the blue into molten cobalt.

She nodded, licking her bottom lip. "I think it's time you made good on your promise to pose for me."

Sixteen

CALEB SAT ON the stool Didi had parked him on in the middle of what she called her happy place. He could see why. One wall was made entirely of glass, bringing in natural light he had read somewhere that artists craved. Hanging along the rest of the walls were prints of van Gogh's *The Starry Night*, *The Kiss* by Gustav Klimt, and one of Claude Monet's most famous paintings, *San Giorgio Maggiore at Dusk*—just to name a few. He silently thanked the art interpretation elective he had taken junior year. So much more useful than pottery making.

While Didi set up a fresh canvas on the easel, he continued to study the space and noticed a theme emerge in her tastes. She loved golden tones as seen in *The Kiss*, the bright orange of Monet, and the stark blues of *The Starry Night*. The paintings on the floor, resting against the walls, echoed many of the colors used by the artists she admired. True to her word during the unfortunate encounter with his father, Didi painted whatever she liked. From still lifes to portraits to something blue, reminiscent of Picasso, she certainly let inspiration drive her.

"Is that the pond from the garden party?" He pointed at a canvas in the corner. The mix of green and blue brought out the bright purple of the water lilies. There was something so serene about the scene, yet it had depth, drawing the eye into the farthest reaches of the canvas.

Didi glanced over her shoulder at the painting. "Yes. I was trying to capture the frog on the pad. He looked like the king of the pond." Her lips quirked into a quick smile.

He searched for the so-called monarch and came up with nothing close to amphibian. "Maybe I need glasses or something. I don't see him."

Exaggerating an eye roll, she padded to the painting in her flip-flops and overalls and pointed at the tiniest speck of green. Unsure of what she had meant for him to see, he hopped off the stool and went closer for a better look. Squinting and staring at the point her finger indicated, he still couldn't make out the frog. Unwilling to give up, he dropped to one knee and leaned closer until his nose practically touched the canvas. That was when he heard the soft giggling.

"There isn't a frog, is there?" He glanced up, catching her failing at muffling laughter with her other hand. Mock growling, he pushed to his feet and yanked Didi into his arms. She yelped and pummeled his chest when he ran his fingers up her sides. The second he hit the underside of one rib her giggles turned into full-on laughter. "Gotcha!"

"Caleb, stop!" she pleaded, squirming in vain to get away from his tickle attack. "Stop!"

"That's for tricking me into thinking there was a frog."

"But you were so serious," she said between gulps of air and breathy laughter. She pushed up onto her toes and wrapped her arms around his neck, taking him into a tight hug.

The second her sweet citrusy scent filled his lungs, he tightened his grip on her hips so she would stay where he wanted her. He loved the feel of her curves against him, like she was made for touching. And crazy as it seemed, he wanted to be the only one touching her that way. He couldn't bear the thought of someone else's hands on her.

Then his eyes settled on her lips when she pulled back to look up at him. He caught himself wondering how they would feel against his own. How she would taste. He leaned toward her.

This was getting dangerous.

"Caleb?"

Her voice pulled him away from crossing the line, and he stepped back, reluctantly letting her go.

As if they hadn't just been about to make out, Didi took his hand and returned him to the stool. Her easy dismissal confused him. Had she felt nothing? Shit. It had been the same at the picnic. She'd pulled away when he began leaning in. If Nathan hadn't arrived with Natasha and Preston, he didn't know what he would have done. Would he have pressed the issue and attempted the kiss like he wanted to do now? But he shouldn't be feeling anything. That was the point of the ground rules.

Frowning at his lapse in control, he sat back down and focused on what he was there for. As part of their agreement, he would pose for her. Exactly what that entailed, he wasn't quite sure. So he asked, "Is there a specific way you want me?"

The mischief he saw so often in her sparked again. "Oh, there are so many ways to answer that question." She picked up a brush and bit down on the wooden end.

"You've got to be doing it on purpose," he accused, narrowing his gaze at her in suspicion.

"What?"

He gestured at her face. "You keep drawing attention to your lips. It's enough to drive a man insane."

"Oh . . ." She pursed her lips and tapped the brush's tip against the lower one. "You mean like this?"

Closing his eyes against the image she'd just seared forever into his brain, he groaned. "You are so cruel."

She laughed again. He would never get tired of that sound, he found himself thinking. He opened his eyes just so he could see the playfulness brightening hers. The urge to pull her into his arms again was so strong it was all he could do to stay still on the stool.

"Just sit there," she said. "You don't need to do anything else. You're handsome enough."

"I knew you were only after what was on the outside," he teased with a self-deprecating smile.

"Just be grateful I'm not insisting on you being naked."

"How benevolent of you." He reached behind him for the collar of his shirt and in one tug it was off and on the floor.

Didi's eyes widened, and her mouth fell open.

It was his turn to laugh.

"Good God." She gasped, pinning him with a stare so direct he couldn't help but stay still. The heat he felt only when he was around her crept up the column of his neck. "I've never seen abs ripple before. Do it again. Laugh!"

Suddenly self-conscious, he said, "I'm not your trained monkey."

"Would it help if I give you a banana?"

He shook his head in dismay. "I'm not going to win against you, am I?"

She winked and gave him the finger pistol. "You're learning. Now sit still and hush before I forget all your rules and jump you."

Instead of complying he struck a pose, making sure to flex so he had definition in his arms, chest, and the abs she seemed to like. Then he said, "Draw me like one of your French girls, Jack."

"What?" She stared at him, mystified.

His eyebrows shot up. "Jack and Rose? From a little movie called *Titanic*?"

"I haven't been to the movies in a while."

"We were still kids when it came out. It's more than a decade old."

"Then why mention it?"

"It was my mother's favorite. . . ." He paused, catching himself at the admission. He hadn't thought about his mother in a while. "Every movie night at our house, when it was her turn to pick, she'd always choose—"

"*Titanic*."

The word struck him directly in the chest. The atmosphere in the room shifted. He could actually feel the air molecules tighten from the tension. As he studied her through hooded eyes, Didi picked up her palette, squeezed a dollop of a flesh tone from a tube onto it, and dipped the business end of the brush into the paint. She considered the blank canvas for a second before the brush landed. Her hand moved with precision and confidence, not a moment's hesitation. He found himself transfixed. Reluctantly he caught himself admitting Didi affected him more than he'd ever thought possible. It scared him. Yet in the pit of his stomach, a thrill mixed with his fear. What was happening to him?

Watching her work was fascinating. One second she would be smiling at something she had done. Then she would frown, pick out a new tube of color or switch out her brush, and continue. Once in a while she would swipe her thumb against her cheek or chin and leave a streak of paint there.

Every time she flicked her gaze at him, his stomach muscles clenched. It was similar to that moment of suspension before the roller coaster plunged down the first hill. He anticipated her looks, but when they came they still sent a thrill through him.

About fifteen minutes later, Didi's frown hadn't stopped. She looked from the canvas to him, then back again. Something must have dissatisfied her, because she removed it from the easel, making sure he hadn't seen the painting by turning it away, and picked up a fresh one.

"Something wrong?" he asked.

She studied him again. "You're distracting me."

He smiled, stretching. "Want me to put my shirt back on?"

Tearing her eyes away from the motion, Didi suggested, "Maybe we just need to talk." She picked up a thicker brush from the set she had bristles down in a jar. "Tell me something about yourself."

"I work out at least four times a week. Anything else you want to know?"

"What's your deal with love?"

His mouth dried up and his throat closed. "You're not pulling any punches, huh?"

"Well . . ." She squeezed a new dollop of paint onto the collection she already had. "You're the one who gave me free rein. Next time set parameters." She pursed her lips at the canvas, then flicked the brush over the center. "So, what's your hang-up with love? I figure something must have happened for you to make not falling in love your number one rule. What, someone break your heart or something?"

Squeezing the back of his neck, he cleared his throat. "Something like that."

"Who's the lucky girl?"

"My mother."

The brush paused midair. She looked at him for a brief instant, then continued painting. "Oh?" was all she said, and yet that one word seemed to have flicked some sort of switch in him, because he started talking.

"I witnessed firsthand what love can do to a person." Grabbing the lip of the stool between his legs, he allowed his shoulders to slump forward. He picked a spot on the floor and kept his gaze there, letting himself remember. "My mother killed herself when I was twelve. It was a shock to everyone because she was the happiest person in the world. Never a smile out of place. I think it was most shocking for my father. JJ loved her. It was in the way he looked at her, like she was his entire world." He swallowed the hard lump that had formed in his throat. "Once, I caught them kissing in the kitchen. My mom had been in the middle of flipping pancakes. The house smelled of cinnamon. I remember waking up to their laughter, and when I

got to the kitchen there they were in each other's arms. Even when they knew I was there sticking my tongue out, because yuck—kissing." Distantly he thought he heard Didi giggle. "Even after they'd stepped out of each other's arms, my father kept looking into my mother's eyes like he was seeing her for the first time."

"What happened?" came Didi's whispered question.

"I honestly don't know. One day she was there, and the next she wasn't. I tried asking my father about what had really happened, but he refused to talk about it. He still does, actually. He'd rather drown himself in work than face the loss of my mother. And he grew . . . cold. Distant. Not even his brother could get through to him. Trust me, my uncle tried. If it didn't have to do with work, he didn't care about it. There were days when we didn't have anything to eat because he'd fired all the staff, and there was no one to go grocery shopping. That was when I started spending more time at Nathan's house."

"Caleb . . ."

He breathed, even though it didn't seem like any air entered his lungs. "That was when I realized all love does is hurt people. It lulls you into a false sense of security, and then *bam*! You slam into a brick wall of pain. A shit ton of pain. Love destroys people to the point where they don't even care who else they hurt in the process." His knuckles turned white, he was gripping the stool so hard. "I promised I would never allow myself to suffer the consequences of falling in love. Never turn into someone like my father because of the pain of losing someone."

Soon after he stopped speaking, fingers pushed into his hair, bringing his head to lean against her. He released his grip on the stool and wrapped his arms around Didi's waist. He

buried his face against her belly. If the front of her overalls happened to get wet, she didn't complain.

They held each other like that for what seemed like the longest time. Yet he didn't care. He wanted the moment to last forever. If only to live within the relief she provided. Her touch was a balm to his pain.

With the resurgence of his grief for his mother and the unconditional comfort Didi gave, one thing became clear. . . .

"My birthday," he murmured after an eternity of silence.

"Your birthday?" she asked back, as if making sure she had heard him right.

He looked up at her. In that instant she seemed unreal. Like an angel sent from heaven to save him. "It's not part of our agreement, but . . ." The words caught in his throat

"But?" she whispered, taking his face in both hands and drying his tears with the pads of her thumbs.

He swallowed. "I would very much like it if you came."

In response, a soft smile graced her lips before she leaned down and kissed his forehead. Then she whispered the three little words he had been waiting for: "Count me in."

Seventeen

THE EVENT FOR the Fourth of July involved games. Couple-centric games. Set against the pretty backdrop of Dodge Cove's man-made lake, with its tall pines and luxury homes surrounding the perimeter. The day couldn't have been more geared toward romance if it were Valentine's Day and not the middle of the year. Standing side by side with Caleb, Didi looked up at the perfect concentration on his face—brows drawn tight and all.

"You sure about this?" she asked with equal seriousness.

He nodded once, then hooked his arm around her waist to grip her hip. The strength of his hold gave her the confidence she needed to grab the back of his shirt. Someone yelled "Go!" In one heave, Caleb lifted her against his side and they took off at a gallop in the three-legged race he had convinced her to join.

Squealing in delight, she let him do most of the work, content to hang on for dear life. The spectators cheered, including Preston, who was jumping in place. He cheered for Nathan and Natasha, their only real competition—according to Caleb. The excitement in the air spurred him to kick faster with the leg currently tied against hers.

Laughter boomed out of her when they reached the finish line at the same time as the twins. They all tripped over one another, but before she could fall, Caleb wrapped her in his arms and twisted so she landed on top of him. Curses and giggles abounded.

She pushed up against his chest, her eyes immediately locking with his. Like standing beneath the eye of a storm, a pause happened between them amid all the excitement and congratulatory shouts. Beneath her hand she could feel the rapid beats of his heart. He sucked in a breath, and in a quick move heaved them both to their feet and began untying their legs.

"Do you think we won?" she asked.

"Yes, we did," he announced.

"I object!" the twins said in unison, already untied.

She still got a kick out of seeing the female version of Nathan. Her femininity put their family's signature dark hair and blue eyes to devastating effect. The female Parker argued with Caleb for the win animatedly, a gleam in her eyes, hands in the air.

"We clearly won by a toe!" Natasha pointed out.

"I have longer legs than you," Caleb rebutted. "So if anyone's winning by a toe, it would be me."

"Yeah, *you*." Nathan poked his shoulder. "Don't think I didn't see you doing all the work, hauling Didi like a sack of potatoes."

"Hey!" she joined in, unable to help herself. Everyone was having so much fun.

Nathan grinned at her. "A pretty sack of potatoes."

She executed an exaggerated curtsy. "Why, thank you, kind sir."

"That's still cheating," Natasha challenged, loud enough for everyone gathered to hear.

According to the mix of jubilation and objection, the crowd was clearly divided. The energy in the air sent tingles of excitement over Didi's skin. She had never enjoyed herself this much. Maybe she had been wrong about these DoCo elites.

"Preston!" Nathan called. "You be the tiebreaker here."

"Boo!" Caleb said through cupped hands. "You know Preston is biased."

"Let's call it even," Natasha suggested, having been reduced to giggles.

"Never!" both Caleb and Nathan shouted at the same time.

Preston suggested a pie-eating contest. This went over well with the mob. In under a minute, Caleb and Nathan sat beside each other on a picnic bench with a pie tin on the table in front of each of them. Natasha walked among those gathered to watch, taking bets, of all things. Didi put herself down for ten on Caleb.

"All right," Preston said. He stood at the other side of the table in front of the competitors, who bumped shoulders with each other. "The rules are simple. No use of hands. The first one to finish eating the pie wins." Then he gave the floor to Didi.

Biting her lip, she glanced at Caleb, who gave her a wink and grin. The combination evoked flutters in her belly. "Ready," she said. Caleb and Nathan shared a look. "Set." She raised her hand and dropped it at "Go!"

The Parker cousins plunged their faces into the pies. Cherry for Caleb and blueberry for Nathan, going with the red, white, and blue color scheme of the party. The crowd cheered for their respective bets.

She danced on her toes, egging Caleb to chew faster. She clapped when half his pie was gone in what seemed like seconds. He moved his face around the tin until nothing was left, then pushed off the table and raised both arms above his head and roared. Half his face was red.

Everyone screamed with him, including Didi. She caught the naughty spark in his blue eyes too late because he was already on her, smearing cherry sauce all over her face. She shrieked and laughed at the same time. His arms around her waist kept her from getting away. In her struggle, Caleb tripped, sending them both to the grass. The breath in her lungs came out in an *oof* and giggles.

Thirty minutes later, with faces washed, she and Caleb entered another game. They came away from the egg toss with second place. Nathan and Preston had joined that one and won uncontested. By the third game, which involved a version of blind man's bluff, where a guy was blindfolded and had to find his girlfriend in a group of girls by listening for her calling his name, Didi had gotten a sense of just how competitive the Parker cousins were.

Caleb had bet Nathan a thousand dollars he could find her in less than five minutes. Nathan took the bet and doubled it. Her head spun from how careless they were being with money. At first she had wanted no part in the silly competition of theirs, but when Caleb had said he would use the money to buy her art supplies, she quickly agreed. If she wanted to give him a painting for his birthday, she needed the supplies. She was running low on canvases. Two grand's worth could keep her painting for the rest of the year. Hell if she wasn't going to take that.

So, standing with nine other girls in a circle and Caleb at the center, she cleared her throat. She needed to be loud enough for him to hear her. Natasha stood behind her cousin and placed a silk scarf over his eyes, tying the ends at the back of his head. Then she tested him by making faces. Caleb merely rolled his shoulders and neck like a fighter waiting for the bell, oblivious to his cousin's antics. Nathan, meanwhile, cued up the stopwatch on his phone and shouted, "Five minutes!" as if Caleb needed a reminder. The taunt earned Nathan the finger.

Didi bit the inside of her cheek to keep the laughter in. The girls had to stay quiet until the game officially started. To add more of a challenge, Natasha spun Caleb in place three times. At his third rotation, Natasha let him go, and the game was on.

All ten girls called out Caleb's name. None of them could approach him. Didi rocked on the balls of her feet, saying his name over and over again. For what seemed like an entire minute, he didn't move from where he stood. He tilted his head one way, then the other. The flutters in her stomach intensified, radiating from inside her belly to manifest as goose bumps on her skin.

Even as she said his name, she mentally willed him toward her. Not because of the bet. Not for all the art supplies in the world. She genuinely wanted him to find her; she wanted to see if he could pick out her voice from nine other girls.

"Caleb!" His name sounded shrill to her ears. The excitement in the air was getting to her. Like a drug, she drew from it, charging her senses to the point of overload. The sunset seemed brighter. The leaves seemed greener, the sky bluer. The air sweeter. She took all of it in like electric shocks running beneath her skin.

At the two-minute mark, Caleb still hadn't moved. She was at the end of her patience. Her excitement had reached a painful peak in her chest. When she called his name again, he tilted his head toward her.

That was when everything changed.

As sure as the sun rose in the east, Caleb turned toward her and walked with confidence until he reached her. Without removing the blindfold, he lifted her into the air. Her squeal turned into giggles. He had found her. Whistles and catcalls rained on them.

"You'd better be Didi, or I'm genuinely screwed," he said, planting a kiss on her cheek.

"Good thing." She yanked off the scarf so she could drown in the blue of his eyes. "How did you do that?"

"I have my talents." He grinned, blinking repeatedly as if to clear his vision.

"You totally cheated!" Nathan accused when he reached their side.

Caleb shook his head, never taking his gaze from her face. "I told you. I can find her in under five minutes. What was the time?"

"Just under three," Nathan grumbled.

"Be ready to pay up." His eyes burned bright. "I'm taking my girl shopping."

His girl.

Those words haunted her for the rest of the afternoon until the sky darkened enough for the fireworks. The party winding down did nothing to alleviate the critters of energy crawling beneath her skin. Nothing seemed to calm her racing heart. She knew she needed to come down, but she didn't want to. The conviction in Caleb's words had worried her. She suspected he hadn't been playacting when he had said them.

When he insisted they walk along the lakeshore, she didn't resist. How could she when he looked at her like she was the only girl at the party? The way the blue of his eyes seemed to shine almost like liquid metal twisted her insides. She let him take her hand. They left their shoes on the grass. The water reaching her ankles cooled her too-hot skin. Today had been too much. More than all the other events combined.

The first spear shot up into the sky. Reaching its peak, it exploded into spider legs of light. Caleb stopped and looked up. She did the same. The next spear quickly followed and spread like a dandelion. The third one popped and sparkled. A kind of choreography emerged. A symphony of blues and whites and reds interspersed with dazzling gold. Soon the entire night sky lit up, blossom upon blossom of pyrotechnic light. The show drew enthusiastic *oohs* and *aahs* while children clapped and laughed.

Since leaving her painting room, he had been different. Less guarded somehow. She couldn't explain the change exactly.

Then, at the height of the show, he faced her. Cupping her cheek, he ran the pad of his thumb over her lower lip. Her breath hitched. She knew she shouldn't. That giving in would be reckless . . . for the both of them. But she tilted her head up in response to his touch. This was the biggest mistake they could make in their fake relationship. She saw it in his eyes too, yet no one spoke of rules when he bent down and took what she offered.

He kissed the way he smiled when he looked at her, slow and easy. Gentle but still demanding a response. And respond she did, tasting the tartness of the raspberry iced tea he'd favored all afternoon. He cradled the back of her neck, tracing the line of her jaw with his thumb as if he wanted to remember its shape.

When he took her bottom lip between his teeth, she wrapped her arms around his shoulders to keep from falling. For a first kiss, amid the fireworks exploding above them, it was amazing. Each pass their lips made tugged at her, begging her to draw him closer. It was as if an invisible string bound her heart to his, and no matter what happened nothing could cut the connection between them.

For the briefest instant, as he whispered her name against her mouth, and she whispered his back, she caught a glimpse of the future. Just a glimmer, not clear enough to see properly. Like a mirage in the desert. It frightened her enough to remind herself their time together was finite. So, after a final brushing of her lips against his, she stepped out of the circle of his arms and looked up at the riot of color bursting in the night sky.

Eighteen

DIDI STARED AT the canvas. Her mind was as blank as the white space staring back at her. Mocking her. It had been a couple of days since the Fourth of July party, and already she had rejected two of the paintings she had finished. One was of Caleb lounging on a picnic blanket under the shade of a tree. The other was of him leaning against his beloved car. None of them would do. They were dull. Flat. Lifeless. Not her usual quality of work. Certainly nothing she was willing to give him for his birthday.

She crossed her arms and scowled. The lack of vision crushed her. This should have been easy. A piece of yummy cake. After that wonderful first kiss by the lakeshore amid a rain of fireworks in the sky? She should be a fountain of talent. A wellspring of all things beautiful. Her muse should be singing with glee. But no. She felt as empty as her mother's gas tank a week before bills were due.

She wanted the present to be special. Something that would show him her gratitude for the wonderful experience he had given her. Getting to play dress up and dipping her toe into his world was definitely a once-in-a-lifetime, bucket-list item for a girl with little to no prospects for the future.

The thought sent her spiraling down. Good luck trying to spark any type of inspiration now. But it was the truth. Everyone in Caleb's world took their future for granted because it was always there waiting for them. The cousins were jetting off to Europe come August. Colleges had practically begged Preston to swim for them, according to Nathan. And Natasha? She had the world in the palm of her hand. Didi? Well, she had until Caleb's party to finish this damn painting. That was as far as she was willing to let herself think.

Her mind wandered away from what she needed to be doing, so she paced. Three steps to the left, turning on her heel, then six steps to the right, then back again. Each time she passed the canvas she would glance at it, imagining the image that would look best on its surface.

Nothing.

A whole lot of nada.

Her feet ached by the time she stopped pacing.

"To hell with it," she huffed up at the ceiling, her hands on her hips.

Picking up her wooden palette and sticking her thumb through the hole, she plucked a fine-tipped brush from the assortment dipped in turpentine and studied the canvas again. Then she coated the brush with yellow paint and brought the tip closer to the blank space. But before she could make contact, her hand shook. Badly. Like eight-point-nine on the Richter scale.

A burst of frustration had her dropping the palette and brush and pulling at her hair, transferring some of the paint on her fingers to the messy strands. A growl climbed up her throat. Of all the days to lose her motivation. She covered her face with both hands and sat on her haunches. She wanted to cry, but her eyes remained dry. All the emotion inside her seemed bottled up, but she wasn't strong enough to unscrew the top.

She had no idea how long she stayed in a seated position with her face covered until the alarm she had set in her room went off. The blaring whine of the digital clock reminded her of one thing: time to take her meds. When she painted, hours could pass without her stopping. Setting the alarm ensured she wouldn't forget.

With a sigh, she pushed to her feet and stomped out of her happy place into her room. She punched the button on her clock and the hysterics stopped. It had seemed louder since she had the house to herself. Although Didi's mother should have been on her way home from her shift at the store by now.

Once silence returned, she shuffled into the kitchen toward the counter where she had left the pill organizer that morning. She popped the PM section for that day and took out the pills. She stared at the collection in her palm.

If she didn't take her pills, she was a hundred percent sure she would finish the painting in time. If she didn't take the pills, just for a couple of days max, her creativity would return. If she didn't take them . . . she would fly until there was no sky left. She was sure of it. Closing her fingers around the tablets that were the difference between life and death, she made the decision. Not hard when Caleb's smile popped into her head. He deserved the best from her.

Light feet carried her into the bathroom. Standing over the toilet bowl, she opened her fist and watched the lifesaving medication plunge one by one into the water. Hand steady, she flushed. The discharge of the water seemed like the loudest sound in the world. It was music to her ears. Around and around the pills went until they were sucked out of her life. She didn't need them. Not right now. She was fine. Absolutely fine. The boat was steady. The kite was flying. And the anchor wasn't tugging too hard. Already she could feel her muse coming back.

She had made the right choice.

A smile stretched across her lips when the front door opened. Like a thief caught in the act, she lowered the toilet seat cover.

"Didi?" her mother called. "Did you take your medication?"

Breathing hard to calm her heart, she said, "Yeah."

The lie came out easily. She could do this. She would have to make sure that her mother wouldn't see her when she flushed the meds. And she would have to pretend to be sleeping. She could do this. It was just for a couple of days, she told herself as she walked out of the bathroom to meet her mom in the kitchen.

"How does pizza sound for dinner?" her mom said, flipping open the box.

Pizza meant only one thing. "Taking another shift at the diner?"

"One of the girls called in sick." Her mother shrugged one shoulder. "It's the dinner rush. More tips."

"That's always good." She tugged on a slice of pepperoni, jalapeño, and pineapple with extra cheese. A weird combination, but it worked. Carbs, meat, veg, and fruit all in one bite. She hummed in appreciation at the salty, sweet, tangy, spicy extravaganza happening in her mouth.

"You're in a good mood today." Her mother bit into her own slice, a string of gooey cheese following in the wake of the pizza.

Excitement bubbled from her insides to manifest as prickles just beneath her skin. "I'm giving Caleb a painting for his birthday."

At the mention of Caleb, some of the light in her mother's expression dimmed. "Oh."

"Mom," she whined. "Don't tell me we have to talk about this again."

Her mother chewed thoughtfully. "It's just I thought I would have met him by now."

"I'm not hiding him from you."

"That's not what I'm saying." She took another bite. "Don't be so defensive."

Didi's shoulders stiffened. Then she forced herself to relax by exhaling slowly. She wasn't going to fight with her mother about this. "Your schedules just haven't meshed, that's all. He spends most of the time at his father's firm."

"But he's important enough that you're giving him a painting for his birthday."

The skepticism stung, but she was determined not to let it affect her. "It seems like the appropriate gift. Personal and made by me. Plus, what do you give someone who already has everything money can buy?"

The ever-present concern that seemed to wrinkle her mother's brow returned. "I just don't want you getting hurt."

"I won't," Didi said without hesitation. "You have to trust that I know what I'm doing."

"You know I trust you. I just . . ."

"Worry," Didi finished for her. Putting her pizza down, she rounded the table and gave her mother a hug, which her mom returned. "After his birthday, Caleb will be off to Europe with Nathan, and I will concentrate on finding a job." The air in the room shifted from tense to comfortable again. "But if you really want to meet him, I can give him a call."

"I guess there's no point if he's leaving so soon. It's not like he's your boyfriend, right?"

The knot in Didi's gut tightened. Did she want him to be her actual boyfriend? The kiss by the lake had made her wish for it. She had learned so much about him in the short time they had been together: He hated junk food. He was athletic and competitive. And he was sweet.

The last part she hoped wasn't just pretend. That the kindness he had shown her had been genuine. To think otherwise would break her heart.

She glanced at the clock hanging on the wall and said, "Aren't you going to be late?"

Her mom's eyes widened. "Ah, crap!" She took one more bite of her pizza, gave Didi a quick kiss on the cheek, and ran up the stairs to her room. "Can you grab my—"

"Uniform's already ironed," she interrupted, raising her voice so her mother could hear her.

"You're an angel."

With a smile on her face, Didi finished her slice and ambled back into her art room. The canvas still remained as blank as when she'd left it, but instead of looking like an empty space, it now resembled possibilities. An infinite number of them. Ideas flitted across her mind's eye, one after the other. It was caused by the excitement of creation. The real effect of not taking the drugs would begin tomorrow morning at the earliest, but she wasn't worried. She had time. With the boost of energy she expected to come, she would have a million paintings completed way before Caleb's birthday bash.

Picking up her palette and brush off the floor, she swiped the tip across the white, creating a bright yellow arch. She tilted her head, placing the brush's handle between her teeth, and grinned. It was a start.

Nineteen

INSIDE HIS CAR, Caleb gently nudged Didi's shoulder. Instead of waking up, she snuggled closer against the door she had been leaning on since he picked her up that morning. She made the cutest murmuring sleep noises. Like a content kitten in a patch of sunlight. She looked paler than usual, which twisted his insides. The dark purple smudges beneath her eyes were also a cause for concern. Reminding himself there was no point in worrying, since they were nearing the end of their time together, he gave her shoulder another nudge.

"We're here," he said softly.

"Too early," she grumbled back, eyes shut tight.

"It's already ten."

"Mmm . . ."

He shook his head and smiled. Then he spoke without

thinking about the words, "Come on, da—" He stopped, shocked. He had been about to call her *darling*. It was what his father used to call his mother. Where the hell had the impulse come from? He swallowed as the rightness of the endearment spread through him. Fortunately her next words distracted him from himself.

"Want more sleep."

"I know, but we're shopping for art supplies today." He took her hand and brought the inside of her wrist to his lips. After planting a kiss there, he moved to the center of her palm, then to each fingertip. Remnants of paint caked the sides of her nails. The girls he was used to were obsessive about keeping their nails clean and manicured. Not Didi. Her hands showed the evidence of her passion. She didn't care who saw, and he appreciated her more because of it.

"That feels nice," she hummed with a sigh. "But coffee is much better."

Laughing, he planted a last kiss on the back of her hand and climbed out of the car. After looking both ways to check that the road was clear, he ran across the street to a café and ordered two coffees to go at the counter. Not knowing how Didi took hers, he filled his pockets with packets of cream and sugar.

Giving the waitress a smile, he left the café and carried the cups back to his car. Once in his seat, he set aside his cup and removed the sippy lid from Didi's. Then he positioned it beneath her nose. As soon as she got a whiff of the life-giving brew, her eyes popped open and she sat up straighter.

"Thank you!" She relieved him of the cup with both hands and gulped down the hot liquid without worrying about burning her tongue.

"Black it is, then." He removed the packets of cream and sugar from his pockets and placed them on the dash. He took one of each for himself and dumped the contents into his cup.

After two more gulps, Didi reached for two packets each of cream and sugar and poured them into her half-empty cup. His eyebrows shot up. She stirred three times, then guzzled the last of the coffee.

"It's official," he said against the rim of his cup before taking a sip.

"What?" She looked at him all wide-eyed and bushy-tailed. Apparently the caffeine had worked its magic.

"I like everything about you. Down to the way you start with black coffee, then end with two sugars and creams." He smiled. "You, Diana 'Didi' Alexander, are the unexpected girl of my dreams." He had meant to tease a blush out of her. Instead he received a scowl so pure it took him aback.

"Let's be clear." She pointed at herself. "I'm no one's dream girl. Especially not yours."

"Didi," he breathed out.

"No! Don't go saying it was just a joke. I see the teasing in your eyes. You're leaving in a few weeks."

"Hey, where is this coming from?" The lovely start to his day had officially ended.

"Remember, you were the one who insisted on the rules. I'm just following them. You're leaving."

Eyebrows pushing together, he set his cup aside again before the remainder of its contents spilled on him. "Yes, I'm leaving, Didi." He looked her straight in the eye. "Nothing will change that." She gasped. If he wasn't mistaken, he thought he had caught a flash of hurt in her big brown eyes. He softened.

"We're here to grab art supplies. Can't we enjoy that? Don't you girls love shopping?"

Her sharp temper flared in her gaze. "Don't patronize me, Caleb Parker." She opened the door and stepped out, slamming it behind her.

Taken off guard by her irritation, he hurried out of the car and barely made it to the shop's door to open it for her. She stifled a yawn with a hand as she entered.

He stepped in front of her, barring entrance to the rest of the shop, then closed his hands around her arms and felt her give in to him supporting some of her weight.

"Are you sure you're up for this?"

She fell against him without actually returning the embrace. "I love the way you smell," she whispered, inhaling deeply and rubbing her nose against his chest. "Like cool water and bath soap. Expensive bath soap. What cologne is that?"

As they stood in the middle of the store's entrance where people passed them by, Caleb realized this girl in his arms was dangerous. She confused him. Excited him. Could break his heart one minute, then reassemble the pieces the next.

Tightening his hold around her, he kissed the top of her head, which smelled faintly of paint, and said, "Why don't I take you home so you can rest? We can always come back tomorrow."

She closed her fists into his shirt and looked up, panicked. "No. I need the supplies if I want to finish your—" She bit down, crushing her lips together.

"My what?" A grin pulled at his lips.

"I already said too much." She pushed out of his arms and straightened. Suddenly her eyes lit up. In another moment of pure transformation, she no longer seemed tired.

"My what?" he insisted.

"Oh, look, they're having an exhibit." She pointed and Caleb turned his head toward a poster taped to the counter. A majority of it featured van Gogh's *The Starry Night*. Besides his *Sunflowers*, it was easily the painting he was best known for. The rest of the poster featured information about the DoCo Museum of Art hosting several of his paintings. Didi used his moment of distraction to hurry deeper into the store.

"Didi!" he called after her. But before he could follow, he paused to stare at his hands. He could still feel the warmth of her in his palms.

After giving the shop owner instructions to deliver everything that same day and taking Didi home, Caleb drove straight to Nathan's house. A nervous tension had settled in his gut since leaving her. He did a quick search of the house and finally found Nathan lounging by the pool with a tablet while Preston did laps.

Taking a seat beside his shirtless and relaxed cousin, he picked up a bottle of water from the bucket of ice between them and twisted the cap off. In seconds he had downed the entire bottle. Still his throat remained drier than sand in a desert.

"All preparations for your party are complete," Nathan said without looking up from his tablet. "All that's left is the execution on the day of. It's going to be an event DoCo will never forget. All parties will be compared to this one. Just you wait."

He felt his insides shrivel up at the mention of his birthday. "Can we talk about something else, please? I have other things to worry about."

"You're harshing my cool," Nathan said with disgust. "I can

feel the stress hopping off your skin and landing on mine. I don't need the wrinkles, so get a grip."

Not acknowledging his cousin's dig, he reached for another water bottle and pressed the cool glass of the Perrier against his forehead as he sighed. It still wasn't enough to alleviate the pounding there.

Frowning, Nathan set aside his tablet and entwined his fingers over his stomach. He kept his eyes on Preston, who had reached one end, tumbled underwater, then pushed off the wall to start the next lap. He sighed, long and slow.

"A hundred laps a day," he said. "Can you believe him? Scouted by all the top swimming universities in the country, and he refuses to make a decision."

"Don't you ever think that maybe he's waiting to see where you want to go?" Caleb asked.

Nathan snorted. "He's being a monumental fool, if you ask me. After your party, the next thing on my agenda is our European adventure. I already have most of our itinerary mapped out. How's the internship?" He turned his head to face his cousin.

"Almost done," Caleb said absentmindedly.

"And JJ is happy with your performance so far? No hitches?"

"When do we ever know if my father is happy? That man is colder than the Arctic."

"We've covered your party. We've discussed the trip. Still you're looking like a confused puppy. What's crawling under your skin?"

Leaning forward to rest his forearms against his knees, Caleb held the bottle between his legs with both hands. The way the afternoon sun glinted off the green reminded him of the gold in Didi's eyes.

"I don't know," he finally said after a long pause. He was afraid to speak. Afraid of what might come out of his mouth. Afraid of the truth he had been denying since the Fourth of July party.

"I don't believe you."

He whipped his head up to stare into the unwavering gaze of one of the few people he trusted. If there was someone who would know what was going on with him, it was Nathan.

"I really don't know," he insisted.

An eyebrow quirked up. "You don't know or you refuse to believe that you already do?"

The question landed like a slap in the face. "I don't want to know, Nate." He hated the weakness in his voice.

Swinging his legs over the side of the lounge chair, Nathan faced him and took the water bottle from his trembling hands. "If you squeeze that thing any tighter you'll break the glass and hurt yourself."

"Nate . . ." He looked into his cousin's eyes, and Nathan's features softened.

"Something wrong?"

Both cousins turned their heads to look at a barely panting Preston. He rested his forearms on the edge of the pool. His green eyes shone bright against the blue of the water.

Nathan smiled at him. "Pres, why don't you go inside and order us some pizza—"

"Chinese," Caleb interrupted. "And lots of it."

Nathan slapped Caleb's shoulder before giving it a squeeze. "Chinese, then."

As Nathan watched Preston heave himself out of the pool, something clicked for Caleb.

"You're in love with him," he blurted out.

"What?" Nathan's face crumpled. "No."

"I've seen that face on the girls I've broken up with. I know what love looks like. That's how I avoid it."

"Then why don't you look in the mirror and see what reflects back?"

"What?" The smugness in Nathan's voice had stunned him. "No."

His cousin grinned. "Exactly."

"No." Caleb leaned forward again and rubbed his lips. He replayed everything that had happened between him and Didi. The laughs. The serious moments. The casual touches. The kiss . . . His stomach clenched. "No."

"People who live in glass houses—"

"Shut up a sec," he said, cutting Nathan off. Then he stood abruptly and began pacing in front of the lounge chairs. "I need to think."

"What's there to think about?"

"This can't be happening."

"I'd say it's already happened from the looks of you."

"No." He rubbed his forehead, not breaking stride. "That's not possible."

Nathan resettled himself on the lounge chair and cradled the back of his head in his hands. "You only think it's impossible because it's never happened before."

Caleb stopped in his tracks. He placed his hands on his waist and looked up at the sky. Its color reminded him so much of one of Didi's paintings. He closed his eyes, and the first thing he saw was the smile on her face when she'd arrived at the garden party in that yellow dress. He could still feel the gentleness of her fingers as they raked through his hair in her painting room after he'd told her about his mother. If he listened hard enough he knew he would hear distant strains of her laughter from the Fourth of July event.

She had completely undone him.

He allowed himself to absorb the realization like the heat from the afternoon sun on his skin.

"Shit," he breathed out.

"Ladies and gentlemen, Caleb Parker, the rule breaker. Can I get a round of applause?"

Twenty

IN NATASHA'S ROOM the day of Caleb's birthday, Didi danced to a pop song she didn't know the title of. The catchy tune was pumped in from magical speakers she couldn't see. How much cooler could this room get?

The elder Parker twin had kidnapped her for some primping and pampering before the party that night. They had worn face masks, painted their nails. There might have been singing into brushes at one point.

"Here it is!" Natasha said as she carried a dress bag into her room.

"Gimme, gimme, gimme," Didi squealed, opening and closing her hands as she jumped in place.

Natasha unzipped the garment bag and pulled it aside to reveal the dress. Didi's squeal turned into a breathy "Oooh."

The sleeveless dress came in a beautiful blush tone. The beads on the bodice formed geometric shapes that were meant to emphasize the body's curves. The V-shaped neckline would skim her collarbones just right. Fringe, the same color as the beads, dangled from the jagged hemline. It was delicate and sexy at the same time. She loved it.

"I think my brother outdid himself this time," Natasha commented, equally as breathless. "You'll look stunning in it."

Didi couldn't stop staring, transfixed by the way the light bounced off the beadwork. "It's so pretty."

But before she could touch it, Natasha zipped the bag right up and laid it out on her bed. "More time to swoon over it later." She took Didi's hand and guided her to the vanity. "It's time for makeup. I will make you so drop-dead gorgeous all eyes will be on you tonight."

Didi's legs bobbed nervously as she sat in front of the mirror. A million clips secured her hair away from her face, which was currently being used as a canvas by Natasha. She rubbed her hands against her thighs. Anxiety zinged beneath her skin like fast cars on the freeway without traffic cops in sight to apprehend them.

Despite the excess energy, fatigue still clung to her like a shirt on a muggy day. She had barely finished Caleb's gift in time. The impulse to get the image just right consumed her, body and soul. The last thing she wanted was to disappoint him.

"Are you sure the painting got there?" she asked for the fifth time.

The pretty socialite smiled at her patiently in the mirror. The bright vanity lights highlighted the elegant lines of her face. She looked like a live version of Vermeer's famous painting *Girl with a Pearl Earring*. So enigmatic. So elegant. Didi had to remind herself not to touch Natasha's face, no matter how much she wanted to. Because that would seem like all kinds of weird.

"Didi, I know you're nervous, but you need to relax or I won't get your makeup just right. Nathan texted me that your painting is in a place of honor among the gifts. Don't worry," she said reassuringly. "When did you start painting?"

Didi shrugged. "Six or seven. My mom brought me along to one of those free painting classes at the community center."

"I'd love to see your work sometime." Natasha set aside the brush she had been using to glide foundation onto Didi's face, then picked up a smaller one for concealer and got back to work.

A blush colored Didi's cheeks. "You really want to?"

"Of course." Eyes bright, Natasha smiled and winked. "Nathan tells me you're really good."

"Come over anytime." Renewed excitement filled Didi. "Would you pose for me? I'd really like to paint you. Your face has such beautiful lines."

This time it was the DoCo princess's turn to blush. "I would love that. Let's set it up. . . . Let's say sometime next week?"

"It's a date!" Didi met the other girl's gaze in the mirror, opened her mouth to say something, but hesitated at the last second.

"What is it?" Natasha paused in her loose powder application. "Is something wrong?"

Didi shook her head so hard she thought the pins in her hair would come loose. "No. It's not that."

"Then what is it? You know you can tell me anything."

Didi took a deep breath and said, "I just wanted to thank you."

Natasha blinked in surprise. "For what?"

"For being so nice to me." Needing something to do with her fidgety fingers, she played with the belt of the silk robe she had borrowed. "You, Nathan, even Preston. You have all been so nice to me." A pinch of sadness entered her heart. "I'm going to miss all of you when this is over."

"Hey." Natasha placed her hands on Didi's shoulders and bent down so their reflections were at face level with each other. Her full lips stretched into a gentle smile. "Who says we can't be friends after this summer ends?"

Didi's eyebrows came up. "Really?"

"Really." She placed a quick kiss on Didi's cheek. "Caleb's lucky to have someone like you in his life. We all are."

At the mention of his name, Didi blushed for a whole different reason. She hadn't seen him in a couple of days. Not because he hadn't been around. Quite the opposite. He had visited her house every day leading up to his birthday party, but she kept turning him away, citing being busy, when all she really wanted to do was take him to her room and make out for the next few hours. Caleb had been gracious enough to leave her alone after checking in on her. He had nothing to worry about, she had told him. Then, after he had left, all she had wanted to do was call him back.

Nathan had made good on his promise of a Roaring Twenties party, Caleb thought as he walked the floor of the opulent ballroom that redefined decadence and excess. Everything was a touch over the top.

The fourteen-piece band delivered jaunty jazz that floated in the air among the strains of conversation. Trumpets blared.

Saxophones wailed. All accompanied by the stunning beats of drums. Snare drums. Bass drums. Drums of every kind. The band members even had choreography depending on the song they were playing.

Gold and silver streamers hung from the ceiling, catching the light from the massive chandelier. Thank goodness it was crystal and had gone with the theme. Otherwise he was sure Nathan would have had it removed and replaced.

Over the dance floor dangled clear balloons filled with gold and silver confetti, like upside-down orbs waiting to pop. No one was dancing yet. Guests were still arriving. But he expected that to change soon with the amount of alcohol being served.

A twelve-foot black-and-white cake with edible pearls sat in a corner. His name was spelled out in gold letters, while unlit sparklers stuck out of the top three layers. Several bathtubs filled with ice overflowed with top-shelf gin. Bartenders dressed as gangsters mixed signature drinks: mint juleps for the men, and champagne punch for the women, since Caleb hadn't been able to decide on just one when asked for his input. Beautiful cigarette girls with their box hats mingled, trays of drinks and hors d'oeuvres hanging from their necks. Table centerpieces boasted more crystals and feathers and glitter.

All that sparkled, all that shone could be found inside the Parker Estate that night.

The guests had gone all out with their attire too. Flapper dresses and tuxedoes indeed. Many of them seemed straight out of grandma's and grandpa's closet. Vintage took on a different name. The women were gorgeous and the men dapper. Cigars were passed around. Cigarettes with long filters too.

One massive table was filled to the edges with gift bags for when the guests left. Knowing his cousin, their contents would follow the night's theme. No matter how much he disliked the mention of his birthday because of all the fuss, Caleb had to admit that Nathan had done a mighty fine job. In his heart, he knew his mother would have enjoyed something like this. He looked up and smiled. Ever since that afternoon with Didi in her painting room, thinking about his mother hadn't hurt as much.

"What do you think?" Nathan asked, grabbing Caleb by the shoulders.

"Baz Luhrmann has nothing on you." He picked up two mint juleps from a passing cigarette girl and handed one to his cousin. "I don't think anyone would mind one drink."

Nathan accepted his and grinned. "A toast," he yelled, and the people nearest them quieted. "To my cousin, for having the good sense to leave the planning to me. Happy birthday, Caleb!" He raised his glass.

A chorus of "Happy Birthdays" came from the crowd as they raised their glasses. Caleb tapped glasses with Nathan, and they both took a sip at the same time. Smiles all around. A great and wonderful energy floated in the air.

"You like it?" Nathan asked, choked up by emotion.

"I know I've been a massive buzzkill while you were planning this, and I'm sorry. You are a genius." He pulled his cousin into a hug and patted his back.

"Oh, good." Nathan discreetly swiped at tears. "Because I didn't get you anything else."

He laughed. "You did good. Proud of you."

A twinkle entered Nathan's eyes. "Wait till you see the fireworks."

"Fireworks?"

Instead of responding, Nathan's gaze moved toward the top of the stairs. As if his body could sense Didi's arrival, Caleb's heart pumped faster. He turned to face the steps to the ballroom fully to find Didi scanning the crowd.

Caleb's heart skipped a beat. She took his breath away in a beaded dress in a color similar to the blushes she got when he teased her. The fringe at the hem moved when she did. The beads scattered down the front caught the chandelier light and sparkled. Drop earrings dangled from her ears while a headband brought attention to the soft waves of her hair. Seeing her all dressed up was stunning.

On anyone else it would have just been a dress, but because Didi wore it, he couldn't take his eyes off her. His father's words about his mother came to mind, *Every time she entered a room the air grew lighter.* He had never understood what JJ had meant until this moment.

As if an invisible force pulled him to her, Caleb handed his drink to Nathan and moved toward the stairs. He never took his eyes away from her.

A step below where she stood, he stopped and took her hand. He brought the back to his lips and pressed a gentle kiss against the soft skin. Her scent comforted him the instant he inhaled. Her presence gave him the unlimited endurance he needed to get through the night. She whispered his name in greeting, and he looked up to see that her smile had softened. It was the smile she reserved just for him when they were alone.

Climbing the last step so he could meet her on even ground, he placed the palm of her hand against his chest.

"You feel that?" he asked.

She nodded, matching him stare for stare.

"It hadn't started beating until you got here."

His words granted him the blush he so craved. "Happy birthday, Caleb."

"Happy now that you're here." He eased closer to her side until his lips touched the shell of her ear. "You look beautiful."

"You like the dress?"

"*Like* is too weak a word for how I feel about you in that dress." He placed a kiss on her cheek. "I almost want to carry you out of here just so no one else will get to see you but me."

"As much as I would like to do that, it's your birthday party. What would they think if we just up and left?"

He frowned and gestured to the crowd below. "They're all too drunk to notice."

She leaned in and kissed him on the lips—a quick, soft touch that ended too soon. "Nate promised really good cake. Can we stay long enough for that?"

"Why, Diana Alexander, are you handling me?" he insinuated with a grin.

She nodded boldly, not bothering to hide her manipulation. Then in a whisper, she told him, "And you still need to unwrap my present."

"Is it anything under this dress?"

Gasping in shock, she slapped his chest. "Caleb Parker, behave."

"You in that dress is making it very difficult."

Biting her soft pink lip, she laced her fingers through his. "Come on, I want to see the band Nate promised."

Unable to resist when her eyes brightened with excitement, he escorted her the rest of the way down to the ballroom floor.

"Why is no one dancing?" she asked, looking at the empty dance floor.

Caleb smiled. "We can easily fix that."

She mirrored his smile and allowed him to guide her to the center of the floor. He pulled her into a gliding step. They moved as if meant for each other. Something in Caleb knew this to be true. Didi was his the same way he was hers. He moved his hand from her hip to the small of her back, closing the already small gap between them. Looking into his eyes, she swayed. He loved the trust in her gaze.

Soon they were no longer the only ones on the dance floor. The band switched to something more up-tempo and Caleb whipped Didi around, then pulled her back in just as quickly. She gasped, then giggled. He knew he would give anything to keep her smiling like that.

The sparkling lights. The mix of cologne, perfume, and sweat. All of it seemed to seep into them as they moved with the mass of bodies. They jumped. They swayed. Didi closed her eyes and twirled in his arms. The fringe of her dress whipped around her legs.

She opened her eyes and beamed. "Caleb! This, all of it!" she said above the music, breathless.

He brought his lips to her ear. "Having fun?"

As if on cue, the balloons popped one after the other, raining gold and silver confetti over them. It was magical. The entire evening was magical.

"So pretty." She raised her hands again, catching the glittering squares in her palms, and bobbed from side to side as he moved his hands up her arms.

A tap on his shoulder from behind broke the spell. He turned around and came face-to-face with the icy glare of the last person he had wanted to see that night.

"Caleb, I need to speak with you," JJ said.

"Father, can we not do this now?" he asked between his teeth. Didi's hold tightened in his hand, giving him much-needed restraint as they stopped moving.

His father's gaze hardened. "Yes, we are doing this now. I'm giving you the option of speaking privately in my study or out here in the open."

Caleb's mouth opened to respond, but Didi's lips on his cheek stopped the nasty words from tumbling out. "Go with him," she said softly so as not to draw attention to them. "I'll be fine with Nate and Tash."

"You sure?" Even if he asked, he already knew the answer, so he caught his cousin's gaze in the crowd. He shared a brief nod with Nathan. But before leaving Didi, he cupped her face with his free hand and gave her the kiss he had wanted since she arrived—hard, hot, and full of promises. Only when she stared back at him with desire-dazed eyes did he let go of her hand and follow JJ to his office.

Twenty-One

"CLOSE THE DOOR behind you," JJ said after entering his office and striding to his desk without as much as a look back.

Caleb did as he was asked, to save anyone else from the words about to be spoken in this room he had grown to hate. He kept his gaze away from his mother's portrait. If only to spare her from having to see his rising impatience at being pulled away from Didi.

"Father, can whatever you have to tell me wait until morning?" he asked. "We have a ballroom full of guests that I must attend to. In case you've forgotten, it is my *birthday*." He emphasized the last word, but barely got a flinch of remorse from the man behind the desk. What else could he have expected?

The smack of a thick folder against wood drew his attention. JJ flipped open the file and scanned the pages.

"Diana Alexander. Seventeen. Father left when she was eight. Mother works multiple jobs to support their family. Grades are deplorable. Barely managed to graduate high school due to a poor attendance record. She's not—"

Caleb's indignation rose with each piece of information about Didi that reached him. "You had her investigated!"

His father pinned him with a cold stare. "It was for your own good."

Caleb ran his fingers through his hair in disbelief, not caring that he messed up the styling for the evening's twenties theme.

"The way you looked at that girl . . ." His father's shoulders slumped when he exhaled. "That's the same way I used to look at your mother. And she's not good for you. . . ."

His father's words snapped him out of his speechlessness. "Don't you dare say that about Didi!"

It took all of his willpower to keep from walking across the room and punching JJ in the face. To actually say . . . No, Caleb wasn't surprised. Of course his father would have resorted to this kind of tactic. Caleb squared his shoulders and faced the bastard head-on so his intentions wouldn't be misunderstood. He modulated his voice, intending for his father to hear each and every word clearly.

"Ever since Mom died, you have buried yourself in your work. You didn't raise me. I had to fend for myself. I dated everything in a skirt so I *wouldn't* become someone like you. Someone who fell in love and allowed it to destroy him." He ignored the shock on his father's face. "Then Didi literally tripped into my life and changed everything. She's the light.

She makes me feel again. Makes me feel like maybe falling in love isn't as bad as I used to think. You should understand that. It's what I remember best about you and Mom."

"Caleb, you don't understand what you're talking about. She's—"

"No!" He waved his hand so JJ wouldn't say anything more. "There's nothing else you can say that will change my mind about her." He turned on his heel and hurried out of the office.

"Caleb!"

Didi had been at the bar with Natasha, laughing at something she had said, when Caleb found her. He immediately entwined his fingers with hers.

"Tash, will you excuse us for a second," he said, already pulling Didi away. She barely had time to leave her glass and say a quick good-bye.

A sense of mischief, like fireworks in her belly, led her to ask, "Where are we going? The party is that way." She hiked her thumb over her shoulder, even though Caleb wasn't looking. He was too busy navigating them toward a secret place only he knew the location of. They left streams of confetti in their wake like bread crumbs.

"Let's go for a drive," he finally said as they entered a long hallway.

"Wow, paintings!" She swiveled her head just to catch a glimpse of the framed artwork hanging along both walls.

"We can look at them later. Right now I just want to get away."

The urgency in his voice called to her adventurous side, and she quickened her steps, the low heels of her shoes clicking against the marble. The end of the hall forked into two paths. Caleb veered left and headed straight for a door at the end.

She barely had a chance to look at where she was going when the unseasonable chill of the air outside nipped at her skin. She bent forward to catch her breath when they stopped along a gravel path. As she straightened she noticed they had made it to the front of the house.

"Which car did you park last?" Caleb asked one of the valets milling around.

"Mr. Parker's roadster," the guy answered, his gaze flitting toward Didi.

"Hand me the keys," Caleb demanded. The entire time he held on to her hand. She wouldn't have wanted to let go anyway. Residual energy from the party still clung to her. Faint strains of jazz coming from inside made her bob in place.

"Sir?" The valet scratched the back of his bowed head.

"Don't worry about it," he insisted. "Nathan won't mind. Just give me the damn keys."

The command in his tone spurred the poor guy into action, grabbing the keys from another valet and tossing them to Caleb. He caught them with his free hand and headed for the end of the long line of cars.

"What's gotten you all revved up?" she asked, matching his pace. "Does it have something to do with your father? Because if it does, I'm not afraid to take him." She made a fist with her free hand and waved it in front of her.

Caleb chuckled, but there didn't seem to be a shred of humor in the sound. "I just want to get out of here and breathe." He rounded the sports car with its top down and opened the passenger door for her. Without further prompting, she slid into the bucket seat. Then he jogged to the other side and jumped in. "Buckle up."

She didn't have to be told twice. She tugged on the seat belt just as he inserted the key into the ignition and started the engine. He pulled out onto the path that led away from the house just as she clicked the buckle into place. He was in a hurry to get away, but all her concern turned into elation when Caleb gunned down the tree-lined driveway leading to and from his house. When she had arrived in a limo with Natasha earlier, her eyes almost popped out of her head at the sight of the massive, almost palatial, mansion. Tash had laughed when she blurted out that Caleb's house was bigger than theirs. A part of her had immediately wanted to explore, see what its walls hid inside. Maybe even see Caleb's room. But she forgot all that the moment she locked eyes with him in a tux. He looked so dashing, like a dark prince from her very own fairy tale.

As they zipped their way along the mountainside, she raised her hands up and squealed. The wind whipped through her hair. She could barely breathe when she screamed for Caleb to go faster. And go faster he did. The rear tires skidded to the side every time they took a corner. Everything around her passed by in a blur—the water on one side and the mountain and trees on the other.

"It's like flying!" she yelled through the engine's roar. "Faster, Caleb, faster."

With a grin stretching his lips, he shifted gears and the car leapt forward like a sleek jungle cat chasing after prey. She whooped and laughed. How could she not? Her belly tumbled like a boulder rolling down a hill. This was the most exhilarating thing to ever happen in her life, and she was with Caleb as it happened.

Because of the rushing wind, she didn't quite catch the words he said when he finally spoke again. She turned to face him. Having escaped from the headband, her hair covered her face. She reached up and tucked the strands behind her ear.

"What did you say?" she shouted at him.

"I think I'm falling in love with you," he shouted back, taking his eyes off the road to look her in the eye.

That one moment was all it took to change everything.

In her periphery a shadow leapt out into the road in front of them. She shrieked, "Watch out!" about the same time Caleb hit the brakes and twisted the wheel all the way to the left. The car swerved violently.

The *crunch* of metal cut Didi's scream short.

Twenty-Two

CALEB GASPED AWAKE, then groaned as pain exploded in his ribs. He grabbed his left side and rolled into the pulsing beneath his palm. Right about the same time, a dull throb began behind his eyes. He shut them again. His body felt like he had bounced off a brick wall after running full speed into it. In the distance, in between the pounding beats in his head, he heard someone call for the doctor.

It might have been a minute or several hours later when sure hands rolled him onto his back again. His breathing went from shallow and fast to deep and easy after a pinprick in his arm. The tight muscles of his face eased with the dulling of the nerves sending protests to his brain.

"Caleb," someone said. "Can you hear me?"

He nodded once. With less pain came more fatigue. All he

wanted was to go back to sleep. What the hell had happened that had him feeling like crap?

The numbness allowed for memories to flood in. His birthday party. The argument with his father. The crazy drive down the mountainside. The crash.

Eyes popping open, he sat up without thinking. Just as fast, hands grabbed his shoulders and applied pressure. He looked around at the unfamiliar faces. Two women in green scrubs and a man in a white coat.

"Where am I? Where's Didi?"

"Caleb," the man said in a calm but firm tone. "You are in the hospital. Do you remember the car crash?"

Losing patience he didn't have to begin with, he pushed back against the nurses holding him down. "That's why I'm asking about Didi." He gritted his teeth as the doctor ran a penlight over his eyes. "There was a girl with me." He reached for her full name before it slipped away. "Diana Alexander. Is she all right?"

"Caleb, I'm going to need you to calm down while I finish my examination," the doctor continued as if his rising panic wasn't about to rip his heart out of his chest.

He grabbed the lapels of the doctor's white coat. "Then tell me what happened to Didi!"

"Caleb, chill!"

It was Nathan's voice that allowed him to let go of the doctor. One of the nurses already had a needle out, no doubt filled with a sedative. Taking deep breaths that ended with a slight twinge of pain, he tried his best not to run out of the private room. The attending physician adjusted his coat and returned the penlight to his breast pocket while the nurse put away the needle.

Caleb turned to where Nathan sat in a corner of the room. He still wore his tux, but the bow tie and jacket were gone and the sleeves of his dress shirt were rolled up. Based on the light slanting in from between the blinds at the window beside Nathan, it wasn't his birthday anymore.

With a frown firmly in place, Nathan said, "Why don't you listen to the good doctor before we start talking about Didi? A couple of minutes. Can you do that?"

Of course he couldn't! He needed to know if Didi was all right. But instead of voicing protestations that would have gotten him nowhere fast, he simply nodded and returned his attention to the doctor. The nurses had left to give them privacy.

The doctor nodded his thanks to Nathan, then studied Caleb. "Besides a couple of bruised ribs and a mild concussion, I can't find anything else accident related. No internal bleeding or broken bones commonly associated with driving into a tree. Consider yourself lucky."

"I will consider myself lucky when I get news about Didi," he muttered under his breath, his impatience rising back to the surface.

The doctor lifted the chart at the end of the bed and started scribbling. "I'm prescribing you a week's worth of pain meds to help ease your breathing. Your ribs will remain sore for a while. I'm also recommending that you stay overnight for additional tests and observation. If nothing comes up, you'll be able to go home tomorrow morning at the earliest."

"Thank you, Doc," Nathan answered for Caleb, who had a

few choice words hovering at the tip of his tongue for the good doctor.

When the man left, Caleb turned the heat in his gaze toward his cousin. "Where's Didi? Is she all right?"

"She's fine. You were both wearing seat belts."

Instant relief burst like a water balloon in his chest. "Holy Christ, I thought I was going to die on the spot."

"Please don't ever do that to me again." Nathan shook his head, the stress on his face obvious. "When I got the call that you were at the hospital . . ."

"I'm sorry." He rubbed his eyes. "I was being stupid driving that fast."

"Consider yourself lucky you had your cell phone on you. Didi was the one who called the accident in."

Holding on to his tender side, Caleb swung his legs over the edge of the bed. A chill down his spine made him look at the hospital gown. "Where the hell are my clothes?"

"Whoa!" Nathan scrambled off his seat and grabbed Caleb's shoulders the way the nurses had earlier. "Where do you think you're going? Just because the doctor says you're okay doesn't mean you should be walking around."

"I need to see her." He hopped off the bed and winced at the coldness of the floor. "I need to see for myself that she's all right."

"JJ's taking care of all that." Nathan's face fell the moment the words left his mouth.

"My father's here?" His eyebrows came together. "And what does 'taking care of all that' mean?"

"Of course he's here," his cousin said without meeting his gaze. "Last I saw him he was speaking with Didi's mom. He's footing the bill."

Knowing his father, the hospital bill wasn't the only thing he was taking care of. He fisted Nathan's shirt and said through his teeth, "First, you're finding me some clothes. If you don't I'll borrow yours. Then you'll tell me where the hell Didi is."

"Jesus, you're pushy after wrecking *my* car." Nathan slapped his hand away, then pointed a finger in his face. "You owe me big for this."

"I know, Nate." He held his anger in check. Nathan didn't deserve it. "I'm sorry about the car."

"The bill's in the mail," his cousin said with a wink before leaving the room.

In jeans and a T-shirt Natasha had brought over for him, Caleb rode the elevator down one floor. He blamed JJ for this. If they hadn't argued, he wouldn't have run out of his office and the crash wouldn't have happened. He needed to see Didi. See for himself that she was fine before he could truly breathe easy.

He wanted to apologize. For driving too fast. For taking his eyes off the road. For putting her life in danger. He staggered and covered his mouth as bile climbed up his throat when the elevator doors opened. He had put her in danger. The mere thought of it made him sick.

"Are you all right?" a woman in blue scrubs asked, placing her hand on his shoulder.

"I'm fine," he said, his words muffled by his hand.

"Are you sure? You're looking pale."

He swallowed several times before plastering a shaky smile on his face. "I'm visiting my girlfriend."

The doors slid shut before the woman could argue against him stepping off.

He glanced left, then right. When he spotted the nurses' station, he approached on wobbly legs. He wouldn't have been surprised if Didi never wanted to see him again.

Stomach in knots, he vowed to make things right with her. If he had to grovel, beg, crawl—whatever—he would.

"Excuse me," he said weakly to the woman seated across from him. When she looked up, he continued. "Which room is Didi . . . ah, Diana Alexander in?"

Her fingers flew over the keyboard of the computer she sat in front of. The frown that crossed her features as she squinted at the screen stopped his heart. Then her words chilled the blood in his veins.

"She seems to be in the psych ward at the end of the hall." The woman looked up at him again. "Only immediate family can see her."

"Why would Didi be in the psych ward?" The question slipped out without Caleb being conscious of it. He retreated into his thoughts. What the hell had his father done putting her in there? Was this his way of keeping them apart?

"I'm sorry," another voice said from behind him. "Did I just hear you inquire about my daughter?"

Stiffly he turned around to face a woman who looked like an older version of Didi, except a mix of age lines and worry lines gave her a tired appearance. She wore a pink uniform of some sort with her brown hair in a ponytail. In both her hands were white plastic bags.

"You're Didi's mom," he said, his voice coming out hollow. He still couldn't wrap his mind around the girl he loved being in a psych ward.

She nodded. "You must be—"

"Caleb Parker. I'm her boyfriend."

"Boyfriend?" The confusion in her face spurred him to explain.

"Didi and I have been seeing each other for a couple of months now. If my father has anything to do with this—"

"Mr. Parker isn't to blame. He's been very generous to us."

"But . . ." His father? Being generous? More like JJ wanted to avoid a lawsuit.

"She's told me about you," she said. "But she said you were friends. From what you're saying it seems like you two are actually together?"

Caleb noticed the purple splotches beneath her eyes and the fatigue in the slump of her shoulders. "I can guarantee that I wasn't drunk when we got into the accident. You can even ask the doctor. My blood-alcohol level was below the legal limit. I swerved to avoid hitting an animal or whatever it was that jumped out in front of us. But that's no excuse. Please believe me when I say I didn't mean your daughter any harm. If I could take last night back, I would. I promise to make it up to her any way I can."

Didi's mother's eyes shone bright with unshed tears. "Caleb, you seem like a nice guy, but after the accident and what your father told me . . . There's something you need to know."

"What is it?"

She transferred one of the bags to her other hand and took his. "Didi has bipolar disorder."

He pulled his hand out of hers. Of all the things she could

have said, this wasn't remotely close to what he had expected. "What?"

"Didi told me this was only supposed to last until the end of summer, right? That you're leaving?"

"That was the original plan."

"Temporary isn't good for Didi. You've already had a bigger impact than you know. I don't know when she stopped taking her meds, but the number of paintings in her art room tells me it's been a couple of weeks at least. This wouldn't have happened if she'd stayed on them. The only reason why she would go off the rails that I can think of has to do with you. I'm sorry, Caleb, but you changed her life in such a big way that she thought it would be all right if she stopped taking her meds. That there wouldn't be consequences. Surely you would have noticed her mood swings. One moment she's as happy as can be, then she's irritable the next."

He nodded vaguely.

When she frowned, her entire face reflected her sadness. "Whatever you think you had with her during this time wasn't real. You fed her mania."

"I don't understand," came out as a whisper.

"Right now she's heavily sedated. When paramedics found her at the crash site, she was practically suicidal, blaming herself for asking you to drive faster."

"But it wasn't her fault." He spoke, but the words sounded wooden to his ears. All the moisture in his mouth had moved to his hands. He rubbed his palms against his thighs to dry them.

"She's physically fine, but . . ." She shook her head. "Caleb, I don't think you know what kind of commitment being with someone who has bipolar disorder is. The medication alone she needs to take . . ."

"Can I see her?" he asked, but deep inside he knew he wouldn't have the strength to move if she said yes. So, when she gave him the answer he was looking for, shame flooded his insides right after the relief he felt.

"I don't think that's a good idea. Best if you just disappear from her life as planned."

Twenty-Three

CALEB CAME HOME in a daze. The painkillers kept his bruised ribs in check but did nothing for the ache in his chest. He didn't know what to do. To give in to Didi's mother's wishes seemed like what he *should* do. But to do so would deny the feelings he knew he already had. Either way, pain was the consequence. So in an attempt to clear his muddled thoughts, he spent hours walking around the estate with no real purpose to his wanderings. No trace of the grand party remained. The ballroom lay as empty as it always did on regular days.

The words of Didi's mother replayed over and over again in his mind. Had it really been his fault that she'd landed in the psych ward? Had he really fed her mania? Whatever that meant. The only thing he knew about bipolar disorder was the mood swings. He suspected that was what everyone knew about it.

He had never met anyone who suffered from it before. And Didi had seemed so . . .

Normal.

He hated himself for thinking of the word, but it was already there before he could censor himself. Her mother had said it would be for the best if he disappeared from Didi's life. But would it, though? Was it what Didi wanted? They had agreed they would part ways after the summer. Just thinking about never seeing her again . . .

He had been so careful. At the first glimmer of love from the girls he had dated, he had cut ties. He had convinced himself that all he wanted was no-strings-attached fun. And of course, the first time he had allowed himself to entertain the notion of falling, this had happened.

Eventually he wandered into the living room. An entire section of the massive space was covered with brightly wrapped gifts—stacked many boxes high. He had forgotten. The party seemed so long ago. Seeing Didi in that dress . . .

A rectangular shape wrapped in simple brown paper and string stood out among the colorful packaging. From its size he recognized one of the canvases he had purchased at the art store with her. His feet couldn't move fast enough. He picked up the gift and tore into it like a child on Christmas morning.

As the string and paper fell to the floor, he held out the painting. Unable to appreciate the picture properly, he brought it to a wall where several still lifes hung. He took one down and replaced it with Didi's work, then stepped back. His heart squeezed like a fist had closed around it.

It was their first kiss. Fourth of July fireworks exploded above them, glittering gold in the night sky of dark indigo and blue. The lake glimmered, reflecting the light show above. It seemed as if the water actually moved. They stood, a little off to the side, in each other's arms. Didi's red, blue, and white dress was a pop of color in the twilight surrounding them. Her face was tilted up toward his, and his hand was on her cheek. He could almost recall the softness of her lips and the sweetness of her taste just by looking at her creation. The brushstrokes were so fine the painting came alive. She had captured the moment perfectly. It showed so much love and emotion.

His eyes welled as he crossed his arms and rubbed his lips. She had given him this. For his birthday. The magical moment they had shared when he finally realized he had let love in. After seeing this, he couldn't just disappear from her life. Not now.

Caleb got into his Mustang and drove straight to her house. This situation between them would get settled once and for all. He had a few things he wanted to say to the girl he loved.

Parking at the curb, he didn't bother locking the car when he stepped out. He strode to her front door and rang the bell. No one answered. Surely her mother wouldn't have left her alone already? He had checked with the hospital. They had gone home. But maybe she'd needed to work. Maybe she'd had no other choice than to leave Didi alone. His heart ached for them. All their money must have been going to filling prescriptions.

No wonder Didi didn't bother thinking about college. And, for the first time, he thanked his father for paying her medical bills after the accident. He wasn't sure if they had insurance. Probably not, considering her mother juggled multiple jobs.

He tried the knob. When it didn't budge, he felt around the

sill for the spare key. Didi had forgotten her keys once and mentioned something about a Hide-a-Key. At the right-side corner,
his fingers skimmed over a rectangular box. Triumph washed
over him. When he slid the container open . . .

No key.

Cursing, he returned the Hide-a-Key to the sill and backed
away from the front door.

There must be another way in, he thought as he skirted around
the house.

The back door to the kitchen was locked too when he tried it.
Why had Didi and her mother chosen that day to be responsible
by locking all their doors? He shook his head and continued
his search for access into the house. This was his first attempt at
breaking and entering, and as much as possible he wanted to
minimize the *breaking* part of the entering. The Alexanders
might not appreciate the extra expense of repairing a window.

When he reached the glass wall of Didi's painting room, he
paused. He remembered the sliding door. Why hadn't he thought
of it earlier?

He approached, hunching like some sort of burglar. He sent
up a silent prayer that their neighbors weren't watching. He certainly looked like the suspicious sort at the moment.

At the door, he curled his fingers into the slot and pushed.
The glass slid open effortlessly. The soft *whoosh* seemed so loud.
He half expected an alarm to go off. His eyes flicked to the heav-
ens. *Thank you, Didi, for not locking this thing.*

Easing the door open just a little more, he slipped inside,
then slid it shut carefully behind him. When he turned around,
his eyes widened. He swallowed, unable to believe what he
was looking at.

Every available space in her painting room was filled with painted canvases.

There must have been at least fifty leaning against the walls, stacked five deep. The easel had a canvas too. And the floors. Everywhere. Canvases upon canvases. From the looks of things, she must have burned through the two grand's worth of art supplies they had bought with his bet winnings. It blew his mind. Didi mustn't have been sleeping at all to amass this much art in such a short time.

What kept him from moving farther into the house were the subjects of the paintings. His eyes darted from each one in quick succession, trying to make sense of it all. Some he even had to move aside just so he could see the treasures hidden underneath. The more he saw, the more his feelings for her solidified in his chest.

There were a couple portraits of him. One while he rested on his elbows on the dock as she walked away. There was one from the garden party while he leaned against a tree with her in his arms. The yellow dress stood out among all the green. Another one was of the Summer Swing. The moment when they were on the dance floor. Didi's first slow dance. Then there was one of their picnic blanket laden with an abundance of food. Several from the Fourth of July party. There were even paintings of his friends. The one of Nathan and Preston smiling at each other was particularly enthralling. She'd even captured Natasha sitting in front of her vanity leaning forward while she carefully applied eye makeup. So much talent. So much creativity in such a short span.

"What are you doing here?"

Twenty-Four

CALEB STOOD FROM his crouched position by a painting, spine ramrod straight. His heart beat in his throat. Slowly, like a burglar caught, he turned to face the woman who had spoken. At the back of his mind he wondered if he should have his hands up in surrender.

Didi's mother stood by the door of the painting room in a peach uniform, fists on her hips and a scowl on her pretty-yet-fatigued face. The years of taking care of Didi were catching up with her.

"Mrs. Alexander," he said, stammering the name slightly. She could kick him out. It was her right, since he had essentially broken into her home. Cops might even be called if she wanted.

His obvious fear softened her slightly, although her

shoulders remained tense when she said, "Call me Angela. Mrs. Alexander makes me sound so old."

He let out a sigh of relief. "Angela."

"So," she said. "What are you doing here?"

Like a criminal confessing, the words fell out of his mouth. "I rang the bell, but no one answered. I figured you were at work and that maybe Didi was asleep."

"If you thought she was asleep, then why force your way in anyway?"

"Please," he begged. "I need to see her."

She rubbed her forehead, shoulders slumping forward, losing all their earlier tension. "What about disappearing from her life don't you understand? You're clearly unhealthy for her. She hasn't gotten out of bed since we got back from the hospital. The only reason I'm leaving this house is I can't miss any more work." The last part seemed like she was saying it more to herself than to Caleb.

"Please, Mrs. . . . . I mean, Angela." He took a step forward. "I love her."

The words came out smoothly. No hesitation. And it tasted right. Felt right. He *loved* her. He would have wanted to tell Didi first. That time in the car hadn't counted since he'd almost killed the both of them. But he knew Didi's mother needed to hear it just as much as her daughter did. He saw that more and more the longer he stayed in Angela's presence. She would do anything to protect her daughter. He wanted her to understand that he felt the same way.

"Her father loved her too," she said harshly. "One bad episode and he left."

He flinched. "I'd like to think I'm more of a man than your husband was."

"Sure, you're confident now. Wait until she spirals again. Let's see how long you last."

Then Didi's words when they were at Coward's Cliff came back to him. "I can't see the future, Angela, but I do know one thing. Whether I stay in your daughter's life or not should be up to her. Just let me see her."

"Can't you see what you've put her through?" Angela indicated the paintings with a swipe of her hand.

From where he stood, he turned in a tight circle. "All I see here is beauty. This one"—he pointed at the garden party painting—"is the first event we attended together. I thought to myself when she arrived in that yellow dress that she was the most beautiful girl there. And this one"—he gestured at the Summer Swing—"was our first slow dance. If she'll have me, I plan on more slow dances with her. This one is my favorite." He crouched down again beside the Fourth of July party painting. "Did you know she gave me a painting for my birthday? It's from this day too. It was of the two of us during our first kiss."

"You don't know what you're saying."

The quiver in her voice gave him hope as he pushed to his feet. "Didi was wrong to stop taking her meds. I get that. Her decision was a dangerous one. I certainly had nothing to do with it. Had I known about her condition—"

"You would what?" Angela interrupted.

"Maybe I might not have dragged her into my world," he said honestly. The admission took her aback. "But I cannot change the past. All I can do is ask for a chance to try to make her happy. You have to at least give me that."

She crossed her arms. Then she stepped aside, reluctantly creating enough room for him to pass. "You're right. Ultimately you being in her life is her decision to make."

With uneven steps, he skirted around the chaos and Angela toward the kitchen. Dishes were piled high in the sink. A mound of clothes sat on the floor beside the washing machine in the small laundry room. The table was a mess of half-empty Chinese takeout. A stale pizza smell hung in the air.

The door to Didi's room was ajar when his gaze finally landed there. Gathering what little courage he had left, he opened the door the rest of the way and peered in. "Didi?"

The mess in the kitchen extended into her room. Clothes littered the floor. Piles and piles of books and magazines ate up what space the clothes and shoes didn't. And there on the bed lay a mound covered by several layers of comforters. The whole scene seemed unreal.

"Didi?" he repeated, unable to come closer without stepping on something she owned.

"Go away," came her muffled reply. The mound shifted with the tugging of the comforters. It seemed like she had curled into an even tighter ball than she already was.

"Didi, I . . ." The walls of his throat closed.

There was a long sigh. Then a tired, weak voice said, "Caleb, whatever you think you're doing here, don't. You said this thing between us would end. Didn't I fulfill my end of the bargain?"

"Yes, but—"

"Then you should go. There's nothing here for you."

"Didi, I—"

"Please," she interrupted. She paused, then whispered, "Just leave."

His world threatened to crumble around him at her words. All because he had let love in. He was so sure she felt the same way. The painting she had given him and the paintings in her art room said so. "D, I'm here for you. Let me be here for you."

"No."

Two letters that made up the saddest word in the world. It sounded so much like *go*. It hit him straight where it would hurt most. His heart. Eyes stinging, he backed away from her room.

Not paying attention, he bumped into the kitchen table and knocked over one of the chairs. Bending quickly, he righted it as the first tear fell. The hopelessness in her voice was what pushed him to run out of the house, not bothering to acknowledge Angela's presence beside the open front door. *She must be happy, getting what she wanted*, he thought. Didi didn't want him in her life. She didn't want *him*.

A new wave of hurt assailed Caleb, crushing his insides. The ground no longer felt solid beneath his feet.

Stumbling to his car, he opened the door and sat inside without starting the engine. He let the tears fall, gripping the steering wheel until his knuckles turned white.

Breathing hard, he found himself starting the car and driving until he reached the Parker Estate. Not bothering to remove the key from the ignition, he stepped out and ran all the way to his room.

Once inside, he paused, fingers combing through his hair. His eyes darted from place to place in search of his luggage, until he remembered where he had left it. He hurried to his closet and pulled down a suitcase and a backpack, then threw both onto the bed. Then he began yanking shirts and pants from their hangers on the rack. Only the essentials. He figured he could buy whatever he needed as he and Nathan went along. The most important thing was getting far away from Dodge Cove. Away from—

"Caleb, what is the meaning of this?" JJ asked indignantly, entering his room.

Good. He needed his father to be just as pissed off as he was. "Did you know?"

"Know what?"

"When you had her investigated." He glared. "Did you know she had bipolar disorder?"

Instead of answering Caleb's roiling anger with his own, JJ sighed. "Of course I knew."

"And you didn't bother telling me sooner?" he roared, barely suppressing the urge to break something. Instead he stuffed shirts into the backpack.

"You ran out of my office before I could. Then the accident happened, and you refused to speak to anyone. . . ."

Caleb gritted his teeth to keep from saying anything more when his father's words trailed off. Did the man have no paternal instincts left? So what if he hadn't wanted to speak to anyone at the time? His father should have pushed his way in. Caleb envied Didi and the love her mother had for her as his fingernails dug into his palm. The pain inside his chest was too much for him to register anything else.

He bowed his head to keep his father from seeing fresh tears and whispered, "If this is love, I don't want it."

"Why are you packing?"

"Isn't it obvious?" He left the mess on his bed and moved to his dresser where his passport was. "Nathan and I are leaving for Europe. I'm staying over at his house until then to finalize our plans."

"Caleb."

He shrugged off the hand his father had placed on his shoulder and returned to his packing. "There's nothing more you can say. I've done everything you asked. I'll see you in a year."

Twenty-Five

DIDI MARKED PASSING time by her mother venturing into her room for food and meds. She must have been doing it in between jobs, because this was the most she had seen of her mother in a while. Didi's latest dark period must have been a doozy if her mom was keeping close watch. She remembered snippets, but most of that time stretched out in a blur spent in the oblivion of sleep.

Caleb had left. Like he promised he would. Why he had come to her house that day still confused her. For a guy who didn't believe in love to say that he might be falling in love with her? His confession the night of the accident had sounded so true it must have been a lie. She'd probably misheard him, because she remembered nothing else afterward . . . not until her mother had brought her home a groggy mess from all the antipsychotics and antidepressants they had pumped into her system at the hospital. She didn't ask about the bills, and her mother didn't say anything. Didi spent most of her time in a tar pit so black no light could penetrate it.

She pushed her head out of the mound of comforters she had been under. Judging from the smell, she hadn't showered in a while. Her hair stuck to her scalp in a ratty mess. The nail polish Natasha had painstakingly applied the night of Caleb's birthday was chipped in several places. Just like the fantasy. It had been fun while it lasted. Landed her in the psych ward, but it had been worth it to be a part of that world. She'd eaten great food. She'd worn beautiful dresses. She'd met new, interesting people who had made her think not all of them were rich pricks and spoiled bitches. Although Amber/Ashley definitely belonged to the fake-bitch side. But that was all over now. Back to her regularly scheduled program.

Caleb's parting words during one of her more lucid moments in the dark hole came to her as she forced her eyes open.

"I'm here for you," she mumbled, curling deeper into the dent her body had made in the mattress from not moving out of the fetal position she found most comfortable. She waited for the nausea that came with staying in bed for an extended period to ease.

The doorbell rang, making her flinch in her cocoon. *Who could it be?* Not Caleb. He didn't seem like the try-again-after-being-rejected type. A soft shuffling to the door followed by a muffled conversation. Her mom was home. Shouldn't she have been at work?

She closed her eyes again as the soft *click* of the front door shutting seemed to echo through the house. Had it always been this quiet? What Didi wouldn't give for some music. Then again putting music on meant getting up. Not right now.

The side of her bed dipped as she was about to drift off again. A gentle hand touched her shoulder. Was it time for meds and food already?

"Didi?"

"Hmm?" she moaned.

Her mother sighed. "Don't you think it's time to get out of bed? You've been camping out in here for too long."

In response, she burrowed farther into her nook.

The hand on her shoulder rubbed soothing circles over the comforter. "That was Natasha just now."

Her ears perked up. "Oh?"

"She said you had plans of showing her your paintings? I didn't know Nathan had a twin. She's pretty."

"Yeah," she mumbled, her mouth dry from not speaking. The inside tasted like something had crawled in and died. She cleared her throat. "I was supposed to paint her."

"Didi." She sighed again. "You know that all I want is what's best for you, right?"

Unable to find any comfort from her position anymore, Didi rolled onto her back. Her eyes blinked open until she locked gazes with the woman who had devoted everything to taking care of her. There were still lines of fatigue on that weathered face, but the purple splotches were gone from beneath her eyes. It seemed she had been catching up on sleep too.

"I know," Didi said with a nod. "And you were right. I shouldn't have agreed to Caleb's proposal. It was one big mess."

Instead of replying right away, her mom picked up a glass of water from the nightstand. Wanting a sip, Didi pushed up to a seated position. She took the glass with both hands and brought the rim to her parched lips. A moan escaped her after a grateful gulp of the cool liquid. Water had never tasted so sweet.

"What?" she finally asked when a pensive expression crossed her mother's face. "Please don't tell me you were fired for staying home too long."

She blinked several times before smiling. "No. I'm still employed. I was just thinking . . ."

"Thinking?" Didi prompted, when it seemed like her mother wasn't going to continue.

"I know you know neglecting to take your meds was reckless. But no matter how wrong I thought your relationship was, I can't ignore the fact that you were happy. That *he* made you happy. I think I made a mistake in asking him to disappear from your life. And I think you'll regret it someday if you allow him to leave. I don't want to deny you the chance to be with him if that is what you truly want."

"Mom . . ." Didi's eyes welled. Was it possible that she had made a mistake by driving him away?

"You should have seen his face when he ran out of here." Her mother's lips quirked into a concerned frown. "I've never seen someone so broken and defeated. I honestly think Caleb's feelings for you are real. The question is: Do you feel the same way?"

The hope in her voice brought Didi back to life like the green grass shooting up from the ground after a long drought ended by rain. "What day is it?"

They both glanced at the desk calendar beside her bed. A red mark circled one of the numbers. During one of their conversations, Caleb had casually mentioned when he would be leaving for his trip with Nathan. Didi had marked it as a way to remember when their fake relationship would be over. It was today.

"I want to go after him," she said more to herself. Then she looked into her mother's eyes. "I don't want him to leave without knowing that I love him."

Smiling, her mother took her hands. "I'll drive you."

"Really?" Didi's entire face brightened.

She raised a finger and winked. "But not before you shower first."

For the entire car ride to the airport, Didi imagined everything that would happen. Like in the movies, she would run out, search for the gate he was leaving from, and make a mad dash, catching him just as he was boarding. He would see her, drop his bags, and open his arms. She would fly into them and pepper his face with kisses. Then she would lean away and tell him she loved him and ask him to stay. His gaze would soften, showing her all the love he felt for her, and he'd say yes, that he would stay. They would kiss again, and the crowd would go wild. Clapping and cheering would drown out the thundering of their hearts.

Unfortunately for her, it wasn't that cookie-cutter.

They got stuck in midday traffic halfway there.

When her mother finally stopped the car by the entrance, Didi couldn't wait any longer. She made a mad dash. The doors barely had time to part when she ran through them. Airport security stopped her before she could go any farther. They'd probably seen her panic and reacted to it. They wouldn't let her go, even after she'd explained that she was running after the guy she loved. From the skepticism on their faces, they must have heard that excuse countless times before.

"Please," she pleaded, breathing hard from her sprint. Her body was still weak from being in bed for so long. "You have to at least let me check his flight schedule."

They pointed at the large digital board to their right. Didi thanked them and jogged toward it. Her gaze frantically searched for his flight number, which she had gotten after giving Natasha a call to reschedule their posing appointment. There were so many flights arriving and departing and delayed and canceled that it took her forever to locate the one she was looking for.

In big bold letters, the board declared the flight DEPARTED.

It sure felt like someone had died.

Her heart sank like a concrete block thrown into the ocean. It didn't matter how sorry she felt for pushing him away when she needed him most. It didn't matter that she loved him. That she had fallen in love with him when he'd kissed her on the lakeshore. All of that was as useless as the countless paintings she had painted of their time together.

Strong hands pulled her into a tight embrace before she could drop to the floor. She buried her face in her mother's chest as the first tears fell.

She was too late.

Caleb was gone.

Twenty-Six

BRINGING IN THE mail after coming home from her new job at the art store two weeks later, Didi kicked the front door closed with her heel. "Mom!" she called as she sifted through bills and junk mail. She headed straight to the kitchen, then stopped. "Are you actually cooking?"

"What?" Her mom waved a wooden spoon coated with sauce as she spoke, cheeky grin in place. "Can't a mother do something nice for her daughter for a change?"

A genuine smile tugged on Didi's lips. Ever since she had come home from the airport a mess, her mother had cut back on her work hours. She could be found at home more often. With Didi's job at the art store, they would be able to make ends meet. Her boss even knew some gallery owners who might be interested in looking at her paintings. Everything seemed to be looking up in her life—except for one part.

She must have frowned, because her mother lowered the flame on the stove with a deft flick of her wrist and wrapped Didi in her arms in seconds. She sank into the hug.

"Thanks, Mom," she said.

"For what?"

"For everything."

"Oh, Didi. . . ." Her mother loved saying her name like a sigh. "You are the best thing that's ever happened in my life. Always remember that."

Heart warm, she hugged her mother tighter. Cutting back at work looked good on her. "You better get back to your cooking before you burn the house down."

Leaving the mail on the kitchen table, she moved toward her room and froze at the doorway. A white box and a note on top of it lay on the bed. Her heart punched the wall of her chest. Her throat closed. It couldn't be what she thought it was. It just couldn't.

Swallowing, she asked, "Mom? What's that on my bed?"

"Oh! It completely slipped my mind. That came for you today."

Slowly, like she was approaching something wild and dangerous, Didi moved closer. She was afraid to blink; if she did, the package might disappear. Once she reached it, she ran a shaking hand over the edge of the box. The smooth texture of the lid seemed real enough beneath her fingertips. She refused to smile. To hope. For all she knew, this was someone's idea of a sick joke.

Drawing a squiggly line over the lid toward the note with her fingertip, she picked up the envelope and set it aside. Not yet. She couldn't bring herself to read what was written on the high-quality paper. Placing a hand on each side, she took a deep breath and lifted the lid. Delicate white tissue covered the contents. But beneath the translucent paper something pink stood out. Her heartbeat reached her ears, and she couldn't seem to get enough air into her lungs.

With just her thumb and index finger, she lifted the tissue—first the one on top to the right then the one beneath to the left. Her breath hitched as she placed a hand against the frantic beating in her chest.

A dress the color of a sunset greeted her. She ran her fingers over the silk—so soft, so smooth. When she lifted it out of the box, the strapless bodice had a sweetheart neckline and the skirt overflowed with tulle.

Her mother gasped, causing her to whirl around.

"Didi, that's gorgeous. Who would send you . . ." She trailed off when she realized the answer to her question.

Hugging the dress against her, Didi picked up the envelope and slipped out the note. The familiar curling scrawl simply said: *Be ready by six.*

She practically jumped out of her skin. "Mom!"

"Didi, no." Her mother shook her head. "Don't do this to yourself again. Please."

Placing the note with the dress neatly on the bed, she went to her trembling mother and hugged her. "I don't know what this means, but I think I owe it to myself to see this through, like you said that day we drove to the airport." She drew back and looked into her mother's eyes. Worry was etched in the lines of the older woman's face. "You just have to trust me, Mom."

At exactly six, the doorbell rang. Didi jerked in surprise, dropping the gold hoop earring she had been in the process of putting on. She straightened and took a deep breath, then picked up the earring again, looking at herself in the mirror. Her hair had grown out a little, so she used clips to keep the strands away from her face.

"Didi!" her mother called from the living room.

"Coming!" she called back, adding the final touches to her makeup. She added one more swipe of gloss on her lips, then rubbed them together with a *smack*. She fussed with the skirt of her dress. Did one last check. This was it. Nothing more she could do but actually show up.

That night, no matter what happened, she wouldn't let him leave without telling him how she felt.

Picking up the matching clutch, her knees shaking so hard she was afraid she would stumble, she strode out of her room and made her way to the living room with all the fake confidence she could muster. Her heart lurched when she spotted Nathan sitting on the couch in a white suit and blue tie.

"Honey, you should hide your disappointment better," he said, getting up and grinning.

Fingers shaking like when she'd first spotted the box on her bed, she patted her hair, making sure the clips stayed in place. "I'm sorry." She hated how dejected she sounded. "I just thought—"

"That I was someone else?"

She nodded, dropping her gaze to the cute ballet flats that had come with the dress. The light in the living room brought out the sparkle in the gold tips. A hand reached out for hers. Nathan placed a soft kiss on her knuckles as she locked gazes with him.

"I think it's time for some fun," he said, squeezing her hand.

She shook her head. "That sounds nice, but I don't think I'm up for it."

"You?" He graced her with that open smile of his. "Not up for fun? Where did the girl who wasn't afraid to jump in, no questions asked, go?"

"Straight to the deepest pits of depression," she muttered.

"Remember what you said, Didi," her mom encouraged, hands clasped. "You have to see this through."

"Thank you, Angela," Nathan said over his shoulder, treating her mother to his devastating smile. "I promise to take care of her."

"Nathan," Didi pleaded with both her tone and eyes.

He wasn't having any of it, tugging her to the open front door. "Your carriage awaits, my lady."

There on the street waited a black stretch limo. She looked up at him as they neared it. "What's going on here?"

"Just get in, Didi," he said, opening the door for her.

Gathering her skirt, she slid onto the low bench and made room for Nathan as he entered with her. Closing the door seemed to be some sort of signal, because seconds later the limo pulled out onto the street.

"Where are we going?" She narrowed her eyes at her too-calm kidnapper.

"Isn't it obvious?" He gestured at her clothes, then his. "We're going to a party."

"Nathan, I'm really not up for this." Her heart shrank to the size of a pea. "Turn the car back around. I want to go home."

"Let's make a bet."

"Why do I get the feeling you're not listening to me?"

His grin was her answer. "If you don't enjoy yourself tonight, then I will leave you alone. What do you say?"

She reached out and shook his hand. "Prepare to lose."

He threw his head back and laughed. "I missed you, Didi."

Some warmth returned to her chest. "I missed you too."

It didn't take long for them to reach their destination. When the limo eased to a stop, Nathan opened the door and stepped out. Then he held out his hand for her. Sliding to the open door, she took his hand and swung her legs out to the pavement. When she straightened, she moved to resettle her skirt, but Nathan beat her to it. He plumped up the tulle and readjusted the neckline.

"I should really be saying 'Hey' right now," she grumbled when his fingers got a little too cozy with her boobs, but she endured the attention anyway.

"Honey, will you just let me do my thing? I came back from Europe for this." He arched an eyebrow at her. She conceded with a laugh. "What the hell did you do to your hair? I didn't want to say anything with your mother there, but . . ." With expert hands, he removed the clips and threw them inside the limo. Before she could protest, he ran his fingers through the strands and shook them out. "You're due for a trim. You've got to do it every six weeks so your hair stays healthy."

She rolled her eyes. "Remind me to put it on my calendar."

His handsome face contorted in a mock grimace. "I should smack you."

The familiarity tore at her insides.

"Nathan," she said, reaching up and taking his hands in hers so he would stop mother-henning her. "You know that this will be just for tonight, right? I don't belong in your world. . . ." She almost said "Without him," but she mentally congratulated herself for keeping it in.

Hooking her hand over the inside of his elbow, he said, "If that's how you still feel after tonight, then I'll honor the bet and leave you alone."

"Then lead the way." She waved her free hand toward the stone steps she guessed they would have to climb.

Bright lights illuminated the front of the Dodge Cove Museum of Art. Its imposing facade boasted massive columns. Large banners depicting one of van Gogh's more prominent self-portraits with his name in big white letters running down the side, hung from each one. The sight made her breath catch. She had only been once, during a school field trip, but she still remembered the pristine marble floors, the cream walls, and the cushioned benches. And the art. The wonderful, gorgeous art. She should have visited more, but life took over.

"What event is being held at the museum?" she asked.

At the top of the steps, Nathan pointed toward the entrance where the guy she thought she would never see again stood. He looked devastating in a dove-gray suit and pink tie. It matched her dress.

Twenty-Seven

CALEB RESISTED THE urge to run and take her into his arms. From the surprise on her face, he could tell she hadn't been expecting him to be there. That might be a good thing. It might be bad. The terrible thundering in his chest told him he knew nothing for certain. His hands clasping the bouquet of yellow roses were damp with sweat. He was pretty sure he was soaking through his shirt beneath his jacket. All this had been a gamble. She had rejected him once before. Her being there didn't mean she wouldn't reject him again.

When Nathan had suggested he be the one to pick her up, Caleb was a hundred percent against the idea. But Nathan had convinced him in that maddeningly persuasive way of his that if he was the one to pick her up, then he could still coax Didi into coming if she was hesitant. This had done Caleb no favors, though, because if he had been the one to pick her up, at least he would have had the opportunity to gauge her feelings. All this for her, and he had come into it blinder than a bat in daylight.

His grip tightened around the flowers' stems as Nathan ushered a speechless Didi closer. This wasn't the time to falter. He knew how he felt about her, and this night was designed for her to both see and feel it.

Unable to take not being near her any longer, he met them halfway. Everyone stopped. His eyes took her all in. The pink dress brought out the cream in her skin, and in the lamplight she was the most beautiful girl he had ever seen. The thought of missing her crippled him.

"Caleb," she whispered.

He swallowed. The sound of his name from her lips snapped him out of his paralysis. With shaking hands, he handed her the bouquet—the color of which reminded him of the dress she'd worn at the garden party. Nathan quietly observed from his side.

Didi didn't make a move to reach her hands out. She just stared at the roses. His heart stopped, disabling him. Then Nathan took her left hand and tugged it toward Caleb. The move encouraged him. He slipped the flowers into her grasp. His fingers touched the back of her hand, sending tingles up his arm.

"Oh," she gasped, then pressed her nose against the blooms. "They're beautiful."

Nathan chuckled. "Mission accomplished."

Caleb endured the shoulder squeeze from his cousin before he left them. As much as possible he wanted to maintain a poker face. He wanted to show her that he was in control, because one word from her could shatter his world. He couldn't allow that to happen. For both their sakes.

He held out the crook of his elbow to her. Every second it took for her to wrap her arm around his was a second he died a little inside. Only when her hand was firmly on his forearm did he start breathing again.

"The museum?" she asked, a twinkle in her eye.

"You said van Gogh was your favorite, so . . ." He faced her with renewed confidence and said, "Diana Alexander, will you go on a date with me?"

A soft flush turned her cheeks as pink as her dress. "Why, Caleb Parker, I believe this is a first for us."

"Is that a yes?"

"That is most definitely a yes."

As much as he wanted to dance in place, he collected himself and entwined her arm with his again. He led her across the threshold beneath the Vincent van Gogh banners and guided her into the marble lobby. Taking her hand, he veered left toward the first exhibit hall. Her eyes widened when she saw the paintings. She let go of him for a moment and danced toward one showcasing children playing.

"Would you believe this is only the second time I've been here?" she asked as she moved to another canvas, this one featuring a mother holding her child.

"Why?" He had to force himself to speak. Her presence awakened emotions in him he had never felt before. Elation at seeing her healthy again. A protectiveness begging him to keep her safe at all costs. Fear she might reject him that night. And the strength to stay until the end, regardless of the outcome.

When she smiled so openly at him, he thought his chest would explode. "Doesn't matter. I'm just happy to be back."

He dared to hope. "Because you're with me?"

"That. And because van Gogh is here."

He stamped down the rising jealousy for two reasons. One, he was getting worked up over a dead guy. And two, she had loved van Gogh long before she met him. So he reached out for her hand. Didi could hardly contain her glee as she entwined her fingers with his. He kissed the back of her hand as they continued their trek deeper into the empty museum.

"Do we have this place all to ourselves?" she asked when they entered the second exhibit space, which featured a collection of still lifes by various masters.

"Until midnight," he said with a tinge of self-accomplishment.

"How did you—" She stopped herself. "Of course. You're Caleb Parker."

"No bills were exchanged during the planning of this date." When she merely looked at him curiously, he rolled his eyes and sighed. "I volunteered here a couple of summers back. I know the security guard."

"Did Nathan help?"

He shook his head adamantly. "If it were up to my cousin, party-planner extraordinaire, the floor would be littered with rose petals and a four-piece orchestra would be playing. This is all me."

She laughed. He had sorely missed that sound too. "You never cease to amaze me."

Her wonder went straight to his heart, spreading much-needed warmth. "We haven't even really started yet." He led her into the room he had a feeling she had been eagerly waiting to see, based on how much she bounced on the balls of her feet.

"Caleb!" She squealed, letting him go once more in order to

run toward the first painting she saw. The artist's self-portrait. "Did you know he used a mirror while painting this? So when you're looking at the right side of his face, it's actually his left."

"Because the mirror reflects the opposite image." He stood at her side, soaking up as much of her happiness as he could.

"Exactly," she said, turning to him. Then her eyes widened, clearly seeing what was just beyond his shoulder at the center of the room. "Dinner?"

He turned around to face the simple table for two with two candlesticks and two silver domes covering their food. Giddy anticipation at what he had prepared grew as he pulled her seat back for her. Once she was seated, he lifted the silver dome to reveal a Big Mac, still in its box, and a bucket of fries, ketchup packets on the side. Didi covered her mouth with both hands, looking up at him with complete adoration on her beautiful face.

"You remembered," she whispered.

He took one of her hands and placed a chaste kiss against her palm before he pulled a cooler out from underneath the table. He produced a liter of soda and presented it to her the way a sommelier at a restaurant would a wine bottle.

"I believe this is the vintage you asked for," he said in a formal tone.

Didi gave the plastic bottle a quick glance and nodded. She waved at the wineglass beside her plate. "You may pour."

A soft *hiss* followed the twisting of the cap. "Would you like ice with that?"

"Please."

He produced an ice bucket from the cooler and used the tongs to add two cubes to her drink. He did the same for his glass but opted for a bottle of sparkling water instead.

"What else do you have in that magic cooler of tricks?" She leaned toward the rectangular box on the floor.

"One last thing." He exchanged the ice bucket for a hot fudge sundae, which he placed next to Didi's fries. "I know you love mixing the salty and sweet flavors while you eat."

Her beautiful eyes that would forever remind him of golden fireworks in a sky of velvet brown misted over. "Oh, Caleb, this is perfect."

"Not yet." He raised a finger. Then he sauntered over to the corner of the room and plugged his cell phone into the speaker jack. After he pressed Play on the list he had put together during the plane ride back, the melodic strains of the Script's "For the First Time" filled the four walls of the exhibit.

"I love this song."

When he returned to her side, he stroked his knuckles down her cheek. "This night is for you."

Awe and wonder flitted across her face. Then, as if she remembered something, hurt settled on her features. His heart broke. "But I thought you left."

"To be perfectly honest, I did." He paused, gathering his courage, then tucked a strand of hair behind her ear. He had to keep touching her, to let himself know she was real, that this wasn't just a dream. "I made it all the way to London, checked into the hotel, and caught myself staring up at Big Ben many days later thinking, *This is my life*. I ran away when what I should have been doing was banging on your door every day with the purpose of convincing you of how right we are together."

"But you know that I'm——"

"Didi, being bipolar is a part of who you are," he said, cutting her off. "But it's not all of who you are. Let me in. Show me all of you."

"Loving me will never be easy."

"Bring it. I'm not afraid anymore." He shook his head to emphasize his words. "I blamed love for the pain I suffered after my mother's death. I blamed love when you asked me to go. All that grief had nothing to do with love. Just because my mother died doesn't mean I love her any less. And just because you asked me to leave doesn't mean my feelings for you have changed. I never would have shown up at your house that day if I thought you having bipolar disorder changed anything." He grinned. "The decision was easy to make after I realized I wasn't willing to lose you. So I got on the next plane back here and organized all this."

"You did all this . . ." She looked around in utter amazement, then returned her gaze to his face. "For me?"

"It was either this or a prom. But this ultimately won out. I wanted something that's just you and me."

"A real date."

His nodded once, allowing the hope he had been suppressing to blossom. "I should have known from the moment I met you that there would be no going back. That I will never be the same. I know now that I'll never recover from loving you, Diana Alexander."

Didi's eyes misted over as she covered her mouth with both her hands again. It was as if she was suppressing all the emotion that wanted to burst out of her. He pulled her hands away from her face so he could lace his fingers through hers. Then, with a slight tilt of his chin, he indicated the open space near their table where benches usually sat. He'd had them removed for the night.

He let go of one hand and executed a bow. "Will you give me the pleasure of this dance?"

At that exact moment, a slowed-down version of Maroon 5's "Love Somebody" came from the speakers. He helped Didi stand and led her to their little dance floor as he had done at the Summer Swing. Without any further prompting from him, she wrapped her arms around his shoulders while he hugged her at the waist. They swayed to the soulful tones of Adam Levine's voice as he sang about wanting to love somebody.

"So if Europe is canceled . . ." She paused, uncertainty clear in her words.

He shrugged. "Well, since Dodge Cove is where you are . . . Loyola actually has several programs I can explore."

"But what about your gap year?"

"I thought that was what I wanted. But I'd rather be with you." He smiled. "We can always travel Europe together. Later, though. I start classes next week."

"I don't know what to say. . . ." She looked up at him with a mix of awe and pride in her expression. Her liking the idea gave him the reassurance he needed that he was doing the right thing. He wanted her to see that his decision, although largely influenced by her, wasn't solely made just for her. He had done this for himself too.

"You don't have to say anything." He planted a kiss on her forehead. "Just know that I love you and will always be there for you regardless of how you feel right now. I'm willing to wait, Didi."

"Didn't I warn you or what?" she asked, grinning.

"What?"

"That you would fall in love with me."

He smirked. "Yeah. Yeah. You were right."

"Good to know." She didn't even pause when she said, "Because I love you too."

Just like everything about her, the confession had come out of the blue. To say he wasn't expecting her to return his feelings with unwavering confidence was an understatement. Even so, never had three words in the English language meant so much. The music, the paintings, the dinner all ceased to exist. All that mattered was Didi and the way she looked up at him like he was her entire reason for being.

"I went after you that day," she hurriedly added. "But when I got to the airport, your flight had already left."

"You came after me?" he croaked out, his throat tightening.

"Yes." She glided her hands to his lapels and closed her fingers around them. "I thought I was too late. That if I'd only realized you were telling the truth about your feelings for me sooner—"

He cut off the rest of her words with his lips. He didn't need to hear the rest. What truly counted had already been said. It took her a second to respond, but when she did she bared all her feelings in the kiss. Her wonderment. Her longing. Her love for him. And he returned each and every one with the same passion, crushing her against him until they were both breathless.

Even though he was unwilling to break the kiss, he had to get the words out or his chest would burst. "You're the first girl I've ever fallen in love with."

She tangled her fingers in his hair. "You're the first boy I've ever allowed myself to love."

He kissed her again. How could he not after those words?

They resumed swaying as Adam Levine asked someone to stay with him tonight. Maybe there was something to Maroon 5 after all, he caught himself thinking while holding on to the woman he loved.

As the last lines of the song flowed between them, Caleb whispered into her ear, "Can you see the future now, D?"

She held his face in both her hands and searched. Arms around her waist, he stayed still, waiting patiently. When she found what she was looking for, her beautiful eyes brimmed— made brighter by the faint light illuminating the paintings. At the first fall, he cupped her chin and brushed the tear away with the pad of his thumb.

She leaned her cheek against his touch and said with a smile, "Yes."

ACKNOWLEDGMENTS

I ALWAYS BEGIN this section by acknowledging family. Without the love and support of my mother, I wouldn't have had the courage to embark on this amazing journey. She has been there through the darkest of times and cheered me on. She is the pillar of strength and courage I strive to be every day. Our nightly walks together are saving graces.

This book came to be during one of the most exhilarating, yet equally painful moments of my life. I would like to thank the Swoon Reads community and all the readers for leaving encouraging comments and expressions of love for Caleb and Didi. Having your support means so much to me. What I know for sure is without your help this story wouldn't have been chosen as part of the third list.

Speaking of lists, I would like to thank everyone seated around the table during that editorial meeting that changed my life forever. Thank you, Jean Feiwel, for that call. The fourth of November will now always hold a great significance in my life. That was the day I met two extraordinary people along with you.

Thank you, Holly West, for everything. I count the days until I can meet you in person and give you a hug. I've grown as a writer because of your awesomeness. Your ninja cutting skills are legendary, unearthing the story beneath the rubble. Thank you for answering all my e-mails. You don't know how much that means to me. Here's to more amazing editorial letters in the future.

This acknowledgments section wouldn't be complete if I didn't take the time to pay homage to the great Lauren Scobell. Caleb Parker wouldn't have been drawn like one of the French girls if it wasn't for you. I can hear those giggles all the way from Swoon HQ. Thank you for putting up with a deluge of private Twitter messages and e-mails. Brainstorming has become so much more fun because I know you're there. Eternal gratitude. I owe you a hug as well.

Thank you to Liz Dresner for those amazeballs cover concepts. Like I mentioned in my blog post, I couldn't have come up with any of them, and yet it seemed like you were reading my mind anyway. You, my friend, I must meet in person.

The editing of this novel couldn't have gone as smoothly as it did without the help of the entire staff of Starbucks in both Paseo de Santa Rosa and Nuvali. You wonderful people kept me caffeinated and motivated. Your smiles and encouragements mean a lot, especially when I have camped out for days on end at one of your tables or comfy chairs. The white chocolate mocha latte or the mocha latte with soy and mint syrup (sounds disgusting but is actually really good) could not have tasted any sweeter without your expert barista hands. Thank you for giving this lowly author a writing refuge.

To all the incredible book bloggers, thank you for your friendship. Kai, the fact that you share my love for BL blows my mind. You are a wonderful person. Precious, you have been there from the very beginning. I am in your debt in more ways than one. Fay, you have to keep writing, girl. That dream is within reach. Camelle, stay strong; I am completely in awe of you. Jas, I know you will forever love Luka, but it makes me happy that you made room for Caleb, too. Louisse, you will always be the best super ninja penguin of them all.

I know I'm missing a lot more people. This is like an Oscar speech where you forget to thank your significant other. If I have left you out, it's not because I have forgotten about you. It's most likely my brain is mush. Leia, thank you for those movie dates and obsessing over TV shows. Your OTPs will live on forever. Meann, I miss you. When *No Love Allowed* eventually becomes a movie, I will make sure Chris Pine is in it if only so we can meet him in person and swoon together. Ron, I miss you, too! Your tweets and Tumblr reblogs never fail to make me laugh.

To Ate Loyce and Kuya Noel, thank you for saving me from burning out. Inviting me on coffee dates or afternoons hanging out with Zoey and Bruno at your house is worth more to me than my weight in gold. You listen. That is enough.

Lastly, I would like to thank God, the powers that be, the universe, whatever you would like to call that feeling of wonderment that comes from knowing there's a force greater than us out there. This book wouldn't have come to be without some sort of divine intervention. It was a spark in the dark that became a magnificent pyrotechnic show in the sky.

Ready for more Dodge Cove fun from Kate Evangelista?
Join Nathan and Preston on their European adventure in

No Holding Back

COMING SOON!

Turn the page for some

Swoonworthy
Extras....

Plan Your Own
Roaring Twenties Party

1. **You will need a theme. Here are some examples:**
   a. speakeasy
   b. gangsters
   c. *The Great Gatsby*
   d. Art Deco

2. **Costumes and accessories are key.**
   a. *Ladies:* flapper dresses, evening dresses, boas, long pearl necklaces, fans
   b. *Gents:* zoot suits, black or white ties on a black shirt, spats (white canvas or vinyl shoe covers), fedoras, gangster hats

   *Just for fun, try flipping things around and let the girls be the gangsters and the boys be the flappers.

3. **You must have cake! Try:**
   a. pineapple upside-down cake
   b. icebox cake or junket (custard made with rennet)

4. **Remember your drinks:**
   Virgin Mint Julep (serves 20)

   - 1 large bunch fresh mint leaves, about 10 stems
   - 1 bottle ginger ale (1 quart or 1 liter, they are approximately the same)
   - 1 c fresh lemon juice or real lemon brand juice
   - ½ c sugar
   - ½ c water

Directions:

Rinse the mint leaves, remove any thick stems, and set the mint aside. Put the ginger ale in the refrigerator to chill. Mix the lemon juice, sugar, and water in a small saucepan. Heat and stir until the sugar is dissolved. Chill the mixture. In a large pitcher, pour the chilled lemon juice mixture over the mint leaves, and refrigerate it for 30 to 60 minutes. Mix together the lemon juice–mint mixture, ginger ale, and ice. Stir vigorously until the pitcher is frosted, and serve.

5. **Decor options:**
   a. Fill a tub with ice and stick all your bottled drinks in there. An easier option is to use buckets and bowls instead of the tub. The sink works, too.
   b. Put flasks and boxes of candy cigarettes out on the tables.
   c. Black-and-white tablecloths add to a speakeasy feel.
   d. Feathers, pearls, glitter, and streamers—oh my! You can place them in goldfish bowls.
   e. If you must have flowers, calla lilies are your best bet.
   f. For an extra touch, place Art Deco posters on the walls.

6. **As for music, it's all about the jazz. The jauntier, the better.**

7. **If you need activities, here are a few to consider:**
   a. Post a doorman who demands the password posted on the invitation before letting people in.
   b. To capture the swankiest costumes and give your guests a memento of the party, take Polaroids or set up a photo booth.
   c. Screen a silent movie like the original it-girl Clara Bow's *It*.
   d. Games like Charleston or mah-jongg can be played, too.

8. **For fabulous invitation ideas, check out:**
   http://www.zazzle.com/
   *Just search "Roaring Twenties Invitations"

9. **And the most important part: HAVE FUN!**
   *Maybe put this party together for your book club while you discuss *No Love Allowed*. ☺

Swoon Reads

Caleb's First-Date Playlist

On the flight back to the States, to keep himself from going crazy over missing Didi and the all-consuming guilt of leaving her, Caleb put this playlist together in anticipation of the date he was planning so he could win her back.

1. "For the First Time" by the Script
2. "Love Somebody" by Maroon 5
3. "Take Me to Church" by Hozier
4. "Miss Missing You" by Fall Out Boy
5. "(Kissed You) Good Night" by Gloriana
6. "Trying Not to Love You" by Nickelback
7. "You're All I Have" by Snow Patrol
8. "Romeo and Juliet" by the Killers
9. "Stubborn Love" by the Lumineers
10. "Girl You're Alright" by Paul Otten
11. "The Shape I Found You In" by Girlyman
12. "Not Alone" by Darren Criss
13. "Overjoyed" by Bastille

It would be a great sound track to have playing in the background while reading *No Love Allowed*. Or, if you have your own playlist that you think fits Didi and Caleb's love story, post it on Facebook, Twitter, or Tumblr and tag @SwoonReads and @KateEvangelista. We would love to listen to what you come up with.

SwoonReads

A Coffee Date

with author Kate Evangelista and her editor, Holly West

"About the Author"

Holly West (HW): Let's start by learning a little bit about you. What was the first romance novel you ever read?
Kate Evangelista (KE): *Suddenly You* by Lisa Kleypas.

HW: Nice. I like Lisa Kleypas.
KE: She's an automatic buy for me. No matter what I'm reading at the moment—I don't even care if I love the book to bits—if she has one that's coming out on that day, I'd be like, "Drop everything! Lisa Kleypas has a new book out! MUST READ." And then I'm dead to the world until I finish that book. I like all her books. She hasn't come out with one in, I think, close to two years, so I'm having heart palpitations just waiting for the next installment.

HW: Do you have an OTP, like a favorite fictional couple?
KE: From *Suddenly You*, Jack Devlin and Amanda Briars. I think it's because she's a writer and he's a publisher, so I'm kind of wishing, "Come on, Universe, do this for me, too!"

HW: This is my favorite question. If you were a superhero, what would your superpower be?
KE: I want my superpower to be the ability to grant wishes. Not as a genie; I don't want to be stuck in a bottle. That would be horrible. I just want that ability to grant wishes. Like if someone had a wish, I'd be able to say "Okay!" and snap fingers and there.

HW: Do you have any hobbies?
KE: I like to bake. And I watch movies. I watch *a lot* of movies.

SwoonReads

Because when I'm not writing, I like to be in that visual state. I still like to watch stories unfold. I like seeing the action, taking apart how that story was told and how the writer would have thought of that. It's still a learning experience and it's like a hobby, but at the same time it's like, "Hmmm . . . how can I use this for my own writing?" But yeah, I bake. I stress bake. So when you see me on social media taking pictures of a lot of baked goods, you know I'm stressed. Seriously, when I had to keep the secret of being on the third list, I baked almost a thousand cupcakes. Almost.

HW: I completely understand. When I was in college, there was one time when I just hit a stress point that was so bad I just walked away from my computer before I threw it out the window, went to Walmart, purchased all the chocolate chips they had and everything else I needed to make the chocolate chip recipe on the back of the Nestle package, and quite literally made a thousand chocolate chip cookies. I had it set up in an assembly line, and I just had all these cookies. I ended up bagging them all and took them to every class I had afterward. I would call people and say, "Bring milk. Don't ask. Just bring milk."

KE: Yeah, it's not necessarily to eat yourself. I don't bake things to eat them. It's the process of baking and feeling useful. And I may have inadvertently given several people diabetes. The conversation went like this: "Cupcakes? Cupcakes? Would you like cupcakes?" "What are you stressed out about?" "I can't tell you. I'm sorry. Have a cupcake!"

"The Swoon Reads Experience"

HW: After you learned about Swoon Reads, what made you decide to actually post your manuscript on the site?

KE: It's so weird because I keep saying that this was really divine intervention. I felt it in my gut that the time was right. Because I kept putting it off and putting it off, and, as I guess you know by now, I write in between projects. I have manuscripts tucked away somewhere that I could just upload anywhere I want with that kind of platform. But you know, you just feel it. It comes to you and it feels right and then you do it. At that time I was like, "You know what? This is it." And I hit publish.

HW: What was your experience like on the site before you were chosen?
KE: Addictive. I love how when you have a comment, you get an e-mail notifying you that you have a comment. So when the comments started coming in and the e-mails started coming in, I was like, "Aaahh! Must go to the website! Must go to the website!" It's addictive. You check it and check it and check it, refresh, refresh, refresh. It's Pavlovian. That whole October of people commenting . . . it was so much fun it's almost indescribable. The way I saw it, even if I wasn't chosen, I loved the fact that the readers were leaving substantive comments. Of course the comments of "I love it, it's great!" were nice, but it's *really* nice when you see someone take the time to write more than a paragraph for a comment just because when they read your story, they were so taken by it, they were so involved with the characters, that it drove them to say more.

HW: Those are the comments that we look for, too. The ones where people loved it enough to really talk about it. You had so many of them that were great. In fact, that was one of the things that first helped us find your manuscript.
KE: It's so nice because even if the comments say "You need to fix this," or "This is what's wrong with it," for me, it's still meaningful that the person was driven enough to actually say those things. Because a lot of people could just be like, "I didn't like it," and stop reading and move on. Instead it's, "I read it to the end and here's

what I thought." And my response is: "Hugs!" If I could hug each and every one of them, I would.

And readers would leave comments on the website, then they would post reviews on Goodreads. They took the cover and put it on Goodreads and were leaving comments and ratings. I didn't even think that was possible because it didn't even have an ISBN, yet it was already there. That was fun.

HW: When you were chosen, how hard was it to keep the secret? I mean, we already talked about the stress baking. . . .
KE: A thousand cupcakes, Holly! *A thousand cupcakes.*

HW: How did you celebrate?
KE: My mom and I ate out, we watched a movie, and then we had copious amounts of Ben & Jerry's Karamel Sutra. And then, after we celebrated, I was like, "Ugh, I have to wait a month before I can tell people!" That was when the stress baking started. I didn't eat any of those cupcakes; I just gave them away. And people were like, "Stay away from me, crazy woman! I don't want your cupcakes!"

"The Writing Life"

HW: When did you realize that you wanted to be a writer?
KE: I started writing in high school because that was when we got our "write a short story" assignment. I remember my sophomore English teacher saying something like, "You know, you have something here." That sort of started the snowball effect of "I was complimented. That means I can do it!"

I got on my dad's electric typewriter—that's how old I am – and started writing. And I didn't care about grammar or format; I just remember typing all my stories out and then binding them on the really nice construction paper, like the hard kind that's marbled— some of them were even scented. Then I would be so proud I'd bring them to school. My classmates would pass them around and read them. I knew I had something when even the girls who bullied me would read my stories. They would swoon over my stories. Bad grammar, bad spelling—I don't even know if the stories really made sense, but people wanted to read them.

But I only really thought about writing as a career five years after college. That was when I read *Twilight*. After *Twilight*, I thought, "If she could do this, I could do it, too!" So I said, "Mom, I'm going to be a writer." And she was like, "Say what?" "I'm going to be a writer!" And she said, "Okay," and walked away. I don't think she believed me until I finally told her, "Mom! I have a publishing contract!" And she said, "What?!" And I was like, "I'm going to be a writer!" I think it took her five years to actually believe me.

HW: Where did the idea for *No Love Allowed* start?
KE: I like to take evening walks at the end of the day. We live up in the mountains and we live near nature, so it's really nice to take hikes. I remember I was taking an evening walk and I was looking up at the stars, and then suddenly this image of a girl falling off a cliff came to mind, and then the boy, who was actually a surfer waiting for a wave, sees her, and swims over and saves her. So that was the initial image. Of course, Caleb—although I think he knows how to surf—is not necessarily the surfer boy who was first imagined for that story.

HW: I know music is important to you. Do you create playlists for your characters or for the book as a whole?
KE: The playlist usually comes after the whole story is plotted out or after the whole novel is written. That's when the playlists come. But there are particular stories, like with *No Love Allowed* and Maroon 5's "Love Somebody," when I heard that, I automatically knew that was the story of Didi and Caleb. That song in particular, that's their story.

SwoonReads

HW: What was it like getting the edit letter? Because I know that my edit letters are really long and I always feel like I have to start with the words *Don't panic.*

KE: I love it! It's like getting a love letter! For me, it really is. It's like getting a love letter from your editor that shows you how you can improve your story a hundred times over. It's basically a road map of examples and pointers. For me, it lessens the anxiety for an author because you just have to follow it. It's like a big load off your shoulders. And we already have something to work with. The novel's already been written. It's not like the editorial letter says, "We don't like the novel. Rewrite, please." You'd be thinking, "Why'd they accept my novel in the first place if they just want me to rewrite the whole thing again?" So yeah, for me it's a love letter.

HW: What is the very best writing advice you've ever heard?

KE: Write the story you want to read. That's basically it. You know that Toni Morrison quote? "If there's a book you really want to read, but it hasn't been written yet, then you must write it." That's always been my philosophy. Would I read this? If I'm writing this, would I read it? That's always been my mantra from the very beginning. No matter what I learn as a writer, I still keep going back to that.

So when I'm writing something and it doesn't work, even if I already have two thousand words down for the chapter for that day, if I'm feeling like, "Um, it's just not working," I will delete and start over. Because it always comes back to, "Would I enjoy reading it?" And as you know, when we edit, it's not just once or twice. You have to keep rereading and rereading until you just want to vomit the story out because it's like, "Ugh, I can't look at this story anymore!" You have to actually love reading it to be able to keep rereading it as you edit. And the reader needs to feel the same way about the book: After they read it, they can't wait to read it again.

No love allowed
Discussion Questions

1. What does the title *No Love Allowed* mean to you? Do you think it fits the overall story and the main conflict between Didi and Caleb?

2. What do you think of Caleb's character in the beginning? How does it evolve as his attraction for Didi grows throughout the book?

3. How would you describe the two main characters, Caleb and Didi? How are they different, and how do their personality traits and interests complement each other?

4. Does Didi conform to your idea of someone who has bipolar disorder? How has reading this book changed your impression of this disability?

5. What are your thoughts on Caleb's relationship with his father? Do you think his resentment toward JJ is justified? How would you handle the grief of losing a loved one?

6. Caleb believes love destroys people. Keeping that in mind, do you think he's right to impose the "no love allowed" rule? That breaking up with someone just because she falls in love with him is the right thing to do?

7. Have you ever considered taking a gap year? If so, what would you do with all that free time? Would you take a trip like Caleb and Nathan?

8. When Caleb presents his proposal to Didi, she warns him that he might fall in love with her. How did you feel when he finally

realizes that her warning has come true? That he broke his own rule without even realizing it?

9. If you were given a chance to be in a fake relationship to attend a whole summer full of fun parties, would you? Why or why not?

10. At the end of the book, Caleb tells Didi that he had to decide between the date at the museum and throwing her a prom because she didn't go to hers. What would you have preferred? Something intimate like the dinner and dancing at the van Gogh exhibit? Or a big party filled with family and friends?

Want to host your own
Swoon Reads Book Club Party?
Download our *free* event kit at
www.swoonreads.com/partykit!

TWO TRASHED REPUTATIONS.
ONE LOVE CONTRACT.
ZERO REGRETS.

JUNE 7, 2016

After a wild party, aspiring law student Taylor's
shiny reputation is screwed unless she can
tame Evan, the bad-boy surfer.

Taylor

Before I even opened my eyes, I knew something was wrong. I wasn't in my bed like I should be, surrounded by the cream duvet comforter that Mom and I had gotten from Macy's last month. The fabric under my fingertips was cool and kind of scratchy.

Evidence number two: It smelled different. Not in a *bad* way. Just not like the apple-cinnamon air freshener that Mom loved and sprayed all over the house, despite the fact that Dad and I hated cinnamon. I usually countered it by walking around the house with vanilla tea candles. As a result, our house smelled sweeter than the largest bakery in town. Ironic, because none of us could actually bake.

I sucked in another deep breath to be sure. Nope, there were no apples, cinnamon, or vanilla of any kind here. Instead, it smelled like cotton with a faint touch of pine and grass.

But the most damning evidence of all was the muscular, bare back of a half-naked—at least I hoped it was just half since I couldn't see beneath the navy blanket wrapped around his hips—guy lying beside me. Who definitely should not be in my *bed*.

"Oh god. Oh. My. God." My voice came out in a hoarse squeak. I squeezed my eyes shut before opening them again. Once. Twice. Over and over until fuzzy stars appeared on the pale blue ceiling—a ceiling that was also not mine—but he wouldn't disappear.

And the stars didn't help my throbbing head. Why hadn't anyone warned me that drinking would make me feel like crap the next day?

With shaky hands, I peered beneath the covers and—*whoosh*—a sigh of relief escaped. Thank god I was fully clothed. If you could call the lacy black tank and capris that Carly had stuffed me into the night before fully clothed. But besides that, everything else looked normal. Except for the strange room and the half-naked guy I was in bed with.

I was in a crapload of trouble. Why had I let Carly drag me to that party last night? (Note to self: Nothing good ever comes from listening to that girl.) But she'd caught me in a weak moment. Granted, I had a bunch of weak moments after I got my wait-list letter from Columbia.

But seriously. Me, Taylor Simmons. Wait-listed! I still couldn't believe it. Didn't they know who I was? Did they even *look* at my application, for god's sake? It was impeccable *and* I turned it in extra early. I even had to add an extra page for my list of accomplishments. For god's sake I should have been a shoo-in.

But the months passed, and no acceptance letter. And they didn't respond to my e-mails and phone calls to check if the computers were down. Or if the acceptance committee was all sick and hospital-bound. Nothing. Until finally, a measly wait-list letter last month.

Anyway, that wasn't the point. Not really. The point was that I'd been dragged to the party . . . and then I'd left. Obviously. But where was I now? And how did I get here? Where was Carly, and why didn't she stop me or—

"Hmph." The guy flopped over onto his stomach, away from me.

Heart racing, I could barely move. My chest tightened, but I didn't breathe, didn't blink, until the soft snoring from his side of the bed resumed. And even then, I could only let out short half breaths.

That was close. Too close. I needed to get out of here. *Now.*

I cautiously eased off the mattress, inch by inch, wincing as the slight movement made my head pound harder. My toes touched the soft carpet, and I pushed myself upright, freezing for a full minute every time the bed creaked. *Only a bit farther.*

After what felt like hours—although it was probably only a few minutes—I slipped off the edge of the bed and took a step toward the door. Big mistake. The floor's creak was like a shotgun blasting across the room. The guy stirred, and I dove toward the ground, landing on the maroon carpet with a soft thump. My head smacked against my forearm. *Ouch.*

What the . . . ? A name was written on my left forearm in my curly handwriting. My name. *Taylor Simmons.* How hammered was I to scribble my own name on my arm? Seriously, what the hell happened last night?

There was no time to think about it now. Still on my hands and knees, I stumbled around the dark room for my silver sandals. The only noise was the soft snoring from the lump on the bed.

Still . . . who *was* my partner in crime? Could it be someone I knew, or was it—holy crap—a random guy I met at the party? Was I a harlot like in those Regency romance novels I hid in the back of my nightstand?

Or was *courtesan* the right word? It *sounded* classier, at least.

"Oh god." I shook my head and resisted the urge to smack my palm against my forehead. Now wasn't the time to get technical.

A sliver of sunlight shone through the top of the window shades, casting a shadow over his face, which was still partially buried in the pillows. I peered over the edge of the mattress but couldn't see more than his muscular, deeply tanned back. I *thought* his hair was dark, but I couldn't be sure. Even though I knew I should get the hell out of here, a part of me—probably the part that was still drunk—hesitated. I had to know who he was. But each time I tried to get closer, the damn floor kept creaking.

Jeez, what kind of house was this?

Against my better judgment, I snooped around the room, careful to crawl on my elbows and stomach like a soldier in enemy territory. Tennis shoes, video games, textbooks with crisp pages that hadn't been used very often, an admirable collection of old-school comic books . . . *Bingo!* I hit the jackpot when I tossed a dirty magazine out of the way and found a stack of pictures. I shoved my tangled, dark hair out of my face and moved a little closer to the light.

Cars and girls. Loads of them. Girls, I mean. And there was a *lot* of skin in most of them. My cheeks flushed hotly at a picture of a girl and the minuscule bikini that could barely restrain her large boobs, which she thrust toward the camera with a coy grin. I couldn't even tell if she was a redhead or a brunette. Just teeth, lips, and boobs. *Flip.* A blond with boobs. Another blond with boobs. A picture of someone's legs on the beach.

"Come on. Show your face," I muttered with a quick upward glance to make sure my unknown partner was still sleeping. He was.

Finally, I found a picture with a guy in it. He was standing in profile, but his face was turned toward the camera, dipped down toward—what else?—more boobs. His nose was pretty straight aside from the teeniest bump at the bridge. Slightly spiky dark blond hair. Laughing dark gray eyes that glanced to the side. His jaw was sort of large, which could be from an overbite, but it suited him. Especially when he smiled. So very hot.

And familiar.

My head jerked to the smooth, lounging back. Now I focused on the tiny glimpse of black Chinese characters trailing down his left forearm. I'd seen that tattoo close-up once before. Everyone claimed it meant "Just live." But for all I knew, it actually meant "Gum lover."

A low groan escaped my lips. No, no, no. Not him. *Anybody* but Evan McKinley, Nathan Wilks High School's very own legendary manwhore. Said to have screwed so many girls that he had to get a new surfboard, because his old one was full of nicks in memory of each new conquest.

Killing any remaining traces of hope that I was wrong, he stretched out his left arm, and I could see his name written on his skin. *Evan McKinley.* In *my* handwriting.

WHERE WERE THOSE DAMN SANDALS?

I crawled around so fast I was pretty sure I'd have permanent carpet burn on my elbows. I didn't care. If anyone caught me within a yard of Evan, the rumor mill would explode. It'd been hard enough to squash the gossip that spread last year when I'd nearly drowned in the Harrison Parks community pool and he saved me. Since then, I'd steered clear of anything that had to do with him.

Which would really suck if anyone knew I spent the night *in his bed.*

Shoes, shoes . . . maybe I didn't need them. Dad had bought them for me when I became editor of the school yearbook. He probably wouldn't even notice that they were missing, but Mom definitely would. She'd been the one who persuaded him to get them for me despite their ridiculous price—you would have thought the crystals were real diamonds—instead of the modest black pumps I needed for my internship at his law firm next year. *You need something pretty! Something fun!* she kept saying over and over. Weird how I was more like Dad, even though I wasn't his biological daughter. The only thing I'd gotten from Mom was her brown eyes.

And she would give me hell if I didn't have my shoes. Besides, I didn't know how far from home I was. And I already wasn't looking forward to the walk of shame I had ahead of me. I wiggled even more beneath the bed, arms spread out in search.

A sleepy male voice laced with amusement suddenly drifted over my head. "They're under my desk."